WITHDRAWN

RIDER OF LOST CREEK

RIDER OF LOST CREEK

A WESTERN STORY

LOUIS L'AMOUR

FIVE STAR
A part of Gale, Cengage Learning

GALE
CENGAGE Learning®

Detroit • New York • San Francisco • New Haven, Conn • Waterville, Maine • London

GALE
CENGAGE Learning®

LIBRARY OF CONGRESS CATALOGING-IN-PUBLICATION DATA

L'Amour, Louis, 1908–1988.
    Rider of Lost Creek : a western story / by Louis L'Amour. — 1st ed.
      p. cm.
    ISBN 978-1-4328-2626-0 (hardcover) — ISBN 1-4328-2626-3 (hardcover)
    1. Western stories. I. Title.
PS3523.A446R53 2013
813'.52—dc23   2012037278

First Edition. First Printing: February 2013.
Published in conjunction with Golden West Literary Agency.
Find us on Facebook– https://www.facebook.com/FiveStarCengage
Visit our website– http://www.gale.cengage.com/fivestar/
Contact Five Star™ Publishing at FiveStar@cengage.com

Printed in Mexico
1 2 3 4 5 6 7 17 16 15 14 13

FOREWORD
BY JON TUSKA

Very early in his career as a pulp writer, in the period just prior to the outbreak of the Second World War, Louis L'Amour created a series character named Pongo Jim Mayo, the master of a tramp steamer in Far Eastern waters. He was in L'Amour's words "an Irish-American who had served his first five years at sea sailing out of Liverpool and along the west coast of Africa's Pongo River, where he picked up his nickname. He's a character I created from having gotten to know men just like him while I was a seaman in my yondering days." After the war, when L'Amour began to specialize in Western fiction, he wrote most frequently under the pseudonym Jim Mayo, taking it from this early fictional character. One of L'Amour's earliest series characters in his Western fiction was the gunfighter Lance Kilkenny, who was featured in two of his early pulp novels. The first of these was titled "The Rider of Lost Creek", appearing under the Jim Mayo byline in the pulp magazine, *West* (4/47).

Leo Margulies was editor-in-chief of the pulp magazines owned and published by Ned L. Pines, which included *West*, a magazine that Pines's magazine group had purchased in 1935 from Doubleday, Doran and Company, Inc. Louis L'Amour developed a close working relationship with Margulies and most of his Western fiction in the 1940s appeared in the various Western pulp magazines that were under Leo Margulies's editorial direction. Authors customarily sold all rights to stories appearing in these magazines to the publishing company and the contents of a particular issue were protected by a composite copyright in the issue registered by the publishing company in its name. Should an author wish to acquire ownership of a story he had sold to the magazine, he had to request an assignment back to him of rights in that story made by the publisher out of the composite copyright in the issue in which it appeared. Upon receipt of this assignment, the author in turn had to submit the assignment together with a registration fee to the Documents Unit of the U.S. Copyright Office. Once that assignment was registered in the author's name, it was incumbent upon him, should he wish to retain ownership, to renew the copyright in the story in the twenty-eighth year following the year of first publication. If he did not renew the copyright, the story then would fall into the Public Domain. The same requirement existed for the magazine publisher. The composite copyright in the issue had to be renewed by the publisher, or his successor-in-interest, in the twenty-eighth year, or the entire issue would fall into the Public Domain.

Louis L'Amour did not request assignments from the magazine publishers for any of his magazine stories, including "The Rider of Lost Creek". Beginning in 1962 his contract with the paperback publisher, Bantam Books, called for him to write three original Western novels a year. In the 1970s, perhaps under some pressure at having by this time to produce so many new books a year, L'Amour turned to making use of his early pulp novels, but changing them enough to make them appear to be sufficiently different so as not infringe on the copyrighted magazine versions. It was by means of such a transformation process that the Louis L'Amour novel, *The Rider of Lost Creek* (Bantam, 1976), came to be published.

I began corresponding with Louis L'Amour when I was at work on his entry for the *Encyclopedia of Frontier and Western Fiction* (McGraw-Hill, 1983). I soon found that the most significant problem I had with him was in trying to prepare a comprehensive bibliography for him. He didn't want the Hopalong Cassidy stories he had written, initially at the behest of Leo Margulies, that were later published in book form by Doubleday & Company under the pseudonym Tex Burns, to be mentioned in any part of his entry, above all in his bibliography. True, he had done those books as work for hire, but he ardently disclaimed any involvement whatsoever in their authorship. He also had a problem with mention of any of his pulp novels that had been rewritten as original Western novels for Bantam. The matter might well have been left there had I not been asked by Thomas T. Beeler, editorial director of the Gregg Press, to take over the job of field editor for the Gregg Press's hard cover Western reprint program for the library market. The titles chosen for this series were all to have new Introductions written by someone other than their authors. My first assignment was to select four original paperback titles by Louis L'Amour for which I was also to write the Introductions. I got in touch with Louis and told him my problem. In order to write four substantial Introductions on these books, I felt it was necessary that we have a long visit with each other simply so that I could collect more biographical and bibliographical information about him. He kindly acceded to my request.

When we did get together, I again brought up the subject of these rewritten pulp novels. Why, I asked him, hadn't he requested assignments on them from the magazine publishers? His answer was that he feared he would be asked to pay money for such an assignment, and without such a payment he might be refused an assignment. "I wrote a novel," he told me, "*Silver Canyon,* for the Thomas Bourgey company. All I ever got paid by them was an advance that came to about three hundred dollars, no royalties. Well, I wanted to sell that story to Bantam. Bourgey told me it was against his policy to assign any copyright back to an author. So I dickered with him. In the end, I had to pay him five thousand dollars to get that book back. I did sell *Silver Canyon* to Bantam, but look how much it cost me to do it . . . just to get my own work back." So that was the last time he bothered to make the effort. It was, he concluded, simply easier for him just to rewrite the stories. However, the result of this practice meant that these pulp novels were never reprinted as he had first written them. It also happened in virtually all cases that, since Louis had never had his pulp stories assigned back to him by the owners, when the magazine publisher in turn failed to renew the copyrights in the issues, the stories in those issues fell into the Public Domain.

Many years later, when Thomas T. Beeler, who had founded the Sagebrush Large Print series in 1995, was negotiating to sell the imprint and the series to Isis Publishing, Ltd., he asked me on behalf of Golden West Literary Agency to help broker the deal. For its part, Isis Publishing, Ltd., wanted to continue buying all of its Western fiction titles from Golden West, as had been the case with Thomas T. Beeler since he had set up Sagebrush Large Print. During the Sagebrush period while the imprint was owned by Beeler, Golden West had introduced a series of new Max Brand Westerns to be published as Circle V Westerns because Dorchester Publishing, a mass merchandise paperback publisher, wanted to do a new paperback Max Brand title every other month and we were only doing four new Max Brand titles a year in the Five Star Westerns. Now, with Sagebrush being published by Isis, it was our suggestion that we include a new Louis L'Amour book every year as a Circle V Western. That is how *Rider of Lost Creek* (Sagebrush Large Print, 2006) by Louis L'Amour first came to be published. This book was the original text of the Louis L'Amour story as it had appeared in *West* magazine and it had not appeared elsewhere since its first magazine publication in April, 1947.

From the beginning the Five Star Westerns have been a first edition series, including restorations based on Zane Grey's holographic manuscripts of novels that were mercilessly edited and changed by Grey's original book publisher. The principal market for the Sagebrush Large Print series since Isis Publishing, Ltd., bought it is now the British Commonwealth. Only one copy of the Circle V Westerns edition of *Rider of Lost Creek* in large print was sold in the American market. Therefore, the decision was made that *Rider of Lost Creek* by Louis L'Amour could be offered in the Five Star Westerns. This would be the first standard print hard cover edition of this novel ever to be published anywhere in the world. Surely that is something that will appeal to the legions of Louis L'Amour's readers who now, as a consequence, will have a chance to read a new Louis L'Amour Western story as the author first wrote it.

CHAPTER ONE

A lone cowhand riding a hard-pressed horse reined in at the hitching rail before a Dodge barroom. Swinging from saddle, he pushed through the batwing doors, slapping the dust from his hat.

"Make it rye," he said hoarsely, as he reached the bar.

When the raw, harsh liquor had cut the dust from his throat, he looked up at a nearby customer, a man known throughout the West as a gun expert—Phil Coe.

"They've begun it," he said, his voice rough with feeling. "They're puttin' wire on the range in Texas."

"Wire?" A burly cattle buyer straightened up and glared. "Huh, they won't dare! Wire ain't practical! This here's a free range country, and it'll always be free range!"

"Don't make no difference," the cowhand who had just entered insisted grimly. "They're a-doin' it." He downed a second shot, shuddered, then glanced up slantwise at Coe. "You seen Kilkenny?"

He spoke softly, but a hush seemed to fall over the room, and men's eyes sought each other questioningly. Somewhere chips clicked, emphasizing the stillness, the listening.

"No," Coe said after a minute, "and you better not go around askin' for him."

"I got to see him," the cowpuncher insisted stubbornly. "I been sent to find him, and I got to do my job."

"What you want with Kilkenny?" demanded a short, wide-faced young man with light hair and narrow, pig-like eyes.

The cowpuncher glanced at him and his own eyes darkened. Death, he knew, was never far away when anybody talked to this man. Along with Royal Barnes, Wild Bill Hickok, and Kilkenny himself, this Wes Hardin was one of the most feared men in the West. He was said to be fast as Hickok and as cold-blooded as the Brockman twins.

"They want guns in the Live Oak country, Hardin," the cowpuncher said. "There's a range war comin'."

"Then don't look for Kilkenny," Coe said. "He rides alone, and his gun ain't for hire."

"You seen him?" the cowpuncher persisted. "I got word for him from an old friend of his."

"I hear tell he tied up with King Fisher," someone said.

"Don't you believe it," the cattle buyer stated flatly. "He don't tie up with nobody." He hesitated, then glanced at the cowpuncher. "I did hear tell he was down in the Indian Territory a while back."

"Who'd you get the word from?" Coe asked the cowpuncher quietly. "Might be somebody here knows Kilkenny and could pass the word along."

"Just say Mort Davis is in trouble. Kilkenny won't need no more than that. He sticks by his friends."

"That's right." The cattle buyer nodded emphatically. "Mort nursed him through a bad time after Kilkenny gunned down the three Webers. Mort stood off the gang that come to lynch Kilkenny. Iffen Kilkenny hears Mort needs help, he'll ride."

"Funny Royal Barnes never hunted Kilkenny for killin' the Webers," someone suggested. "With Barnes bein' half-brother to the Webers and all."

"That'd be somethin' . . . Barnes an' Kilkenny," another agreed. "Two of the fastest gunmen in the West."

Conversation flowered in the room, and through it all the

name of Kilkenny was woven like a scarlet thread. One man had seen him in Abilene. Two men had cornered him there, two bad men trying to build a tough reputation. They had drawn, but both had died before they could fire a shot. Another man said he had seen Kilkenny hold his hand out at arm's length with a poker chip on its back. Then he had tipped his hand slowly, and, when the chip fell free, he had drawn and fired before the chip reached the level of his waist.

"He's faster'n Hickok," someone else said dogmatically, "and he's got the nerve of Ben Thompson."

"What's he look like?" still another demanded. "I never seen the feller."

"Nobody agrees," the cattle buyer said. "I've heard a dozen descriptions of Kilkenny, and no two alike. He never makes hisself known until the guns start shootin', and he fades right after. Nobody knows him."

"This wire won't last in Texas," a lean, raw-boned Texan changed the subject to say. "That Live Oaks country nor this 'n', either, they ain't made for wire. It's free range and always will be. The buffalo was here before the longhorn, and it was free grass then. It always has been."

"I don't know," someone else said doubtfully. "There's farmers comin' out from the East. Hoemen who'll fence their own ground and break the sod for crops."

"This country ain't right for farmin', I tell you," a young cowhand said. "You ever foller a trail herd? Iffen they ever plow this plains country up, it will blow clean to Mexico!"

But even as the men in Dodge talked and condemned wires, along the right of way in Botalla, in the Live Oak country, lay huge reels of it, gleaming and new. Literally miles of it, on great spools, unloaded from wagon trains and ready to be strung. Reports implied there would soon be a railroad in Texas. Fat beef, good beef, would soon be in great demand. In this year of

1880, forty thousand tons of steel barbed wire of the Haish and Glidden Star varieties were to be sold to Texas ranchmen.

In the bar of the old Trail House in Botalla, rancher Webb Steele smashed a ham-like fist upon the bar. "We're puttin' it up!" he shouted. "Hoss high, pig tight, and bull strong! If them who don't like it want war, it's war they'll get!"

"Who fences Lost Creek Valley?" some hardened soul demanded. "You or Chet Lord?"

"I'm fencin' it!" Steele declared, glaring about the room. "And if necessary my riders will ride the fence with rifles!"

Outside the barroom a tall man in black trousers, black shirt, and a worn buckskin vest walked a rangy yellow horse down the one street of Botalla, then swung down in front of the Trail House. The buckskin relaxed, standing three-legged, head hanging in weariness. The tall man loosened the cinch, taking in the street with quick, alert eyes.

It was merely the usual double row of false-fronted buildings he saw, almost every other one a saloon. He knew that men along the walk were looking at him, wondering about him, but he seemed not to notice.

He could feel their eyes, though, like a tangible touch, lifting from his low-slung, tied-down guns to his lean brown face and green eyes. They were noting the dust in the grain of his face, the dust on his clothing, the dust on the long-legged buckskin. They would know he had traveled far and fast, and that would mean he had traveled for a reason.

When he stepped up on the walk, he closed his eyes for an instant. It was a trick he had learned that would leave his eyes accustomed to inner dimness much more quickly than would otherwise be the case. Then he stepped through the doors, letting his eyes shift from left to right, taking in the room in one swift, comprehensive glance. There was no one he knew. No one here, he was sure, knew him.

Webb Steele, brawny and huge, strode past him through the doors, his guns seeming small, buckled to his massive frame.

"I'll have a whiskey," the tall man said to the bartender. He took off his flat-crowned black hat to run his fingers around the sweaty band, then through his black curly hair. He replaced the hat, dropped his right hand to the bar, then glanced about.

Several men leaned on the bar nearby. The nearest, a man who had walked to the bar as Steele left, was a slim, wiry young fellow in a fringed buckskin jacket and black jeans stuffed into cowhide boots.

The young man had gray, cold eyes. He looked hard at the stranger. "Don't I know you?" he demanded.

The green eyes lifted in a direct expressionless look. "You might."

"Ridin' through?"

"Mebbe."

"Want a job?"

"Mebbe."

"Ain't you a cowhand?"

"Sometimes."

"I'll pay well."

"What outfit you with?"

"I'm not with any outfit," the young man said sharply. "I *am* the Tumblin' R."

"Yeah?"

The young man's face flamed and a queer, white eagerness came into his eyes. "I don't like the way you said that!" he snapped.

"Does it matter?" drawled the tall man. For an instant the young rancher stared as if he couldn't believe his ears, and he heard men hurriedly backing away from him. Something turned over inside him, and with a sickening sensation in the pit of his stomach he realized with startling clarity that he was facing a gun battle, out in the open and alone.

An icy chill went down his spine. Always before when he had talked, loud and free, the fact that he was Chet Lord's son had saved him. Men knew his hard-bitten old father only too well. Then, there had been Bonner and Swindell. Those two men had affronted Steve Lord and later both had been found dead in the trail, gun in hand.

Suddenly the awful realization that he must fight swept over Steve Lord. Nothing his father might do afterward would do any good now. He stiffened. His face was tense and white as he stared into the cold green eyes of the stranger.

"Yeah," he snapped, "it matters, and I'll make it matter!"

His hand hovered over his gun. For an instant, the watchers held their breaths. The tall man at the bar stared at Steve Lord coolly, then Steve saw those hard green eyes change, and a glint of humor and friendliness came into them.

With a shrug the stranger turned away. "Well," he drawled, "don't kill me now. I hate to get shot on an empty stomach." Deliberately he turned his back and looked at the bartender. "How about another whiskey? The trail shore does make a feller dry."

Everyone began talking suddenly, and Steve Lord, astonished and relieved, dropped his hand to his side. Something had happened to him and all he knew was that he had narrowly escaped death from a shoot-out with a man to whom blazing guns were not new.

The tall man at the bar lifted his eyes to the mirror in time to see a thin-bodied fellow with close-set eyes slide quietly from his chair and go out the side door. No one seemed to notice him go except the tall stranger who noted the intentness of the man's eyes, and something sly in his movements.

The stranger swallowed his drink, turned on his heel, and walked outside. The thin man who had left the Trail House was talking with three men across the street in front of the Spur Saloon. The tall man saw the eyes of the three pick him up. Swiftly screening their faces, he strolled on.

Idling in front of the empty stage station a few minutes later, he saw Steve Lord coming toward him. Something about the young man disturbed him, but although his eyes lifted from the cigarette he was rolling, he said nothing when Steve stopped before him.

"You could have killed me," Steve said sharply, staring at him.

"Yeah." The tall stranger smiled a little.

"Why didn't you? I made a fool of myself, talkin' too much."

The stranger smiled. "No use killin' a man unnecessarily. You may be Chet Lord's son as I heard, but I think you make your own tracks."

"Thanks. That's the first time anybody ever said that to me."

"Mebbe they should have." The stranger took a long drag, and glanced sideward at Steve. "Knowin' you're pretty much of a man often helps a feller be one."

"Who are you?" asked Steve Lord.

The stranger shrugged. "The name is Lance," he replied slowly. "Is that enough for you?"

"Yeah. About that job. We'd like to have you. I may not be gun slick but I know when a man is."

"I don't reckon I'll go to work just now," observed the man who said his name was Lance.

"I'd rather have you on our side than the other," Steve said honestly. "And we'll pay well."

"Mebbe I won't ride for either side."

"You got to! Those that ain't for us are against us."

Lance smoked quietly for a moment. "Tell me," he finally said, "what kind of a scrap is this?"

"It's a three-cornered scrap actually," Steve said. "Our outfit has about forty riders, and Webb Steele has about the same number. We split the Live Oak country between us. By the Live Oak, I mean the territory between the two ranges of hills you see out east and west of here. They taper down to a point at the border. Webb Steele and us Lords both have started puttin' up wire, and no trouble till we get to Lost Creek Valley, the richest piece of it all. Good grass there, and lots of water."

"You said it was three-cornered. Who's the other corner?"

"He don't matter so much." Steve shrugged. "The real fight is between the two big outfits. This other corner is a feller name of Mort Davis. Squatter. He come in here about three year ago with his family and squatted on the Wagontire water hole. We cut his wire, and he cut ours. There she stands right now."

Lance studied the street thoughtfully, aware that while he was talking with Steve Lord, something was building up down there. Something that smelled like trouble. The three men with whom the thin man had talked had scattered. One was watching a boy unloading some feed, one was leaning on the hitch rail, another was studying some faded medicine show posters in a window.

Abruptly Lance turned away from Steve. There was something behind this, and he intended to know what. If they wanted him, they could have him.

CHAPTER TWO

Lance had started strolling carelessly toward the Spur Saloon when he heard a sudden rattle of wheels and racing hoofs behind him, and sprang aside just in time to escape being run down by a madly careening buckboard. The driver—a girl—stood up, sawing the plunging broncos to a halt, then wheeling the buckboard to race them back at a spanking trot. She brought them up alongside of Lance and her eyes were ablaze with irritation.

"Will you please stay out of the street?" she demanded icily.

Lance looked at her steadily. Red-gold hair blew in the wind, and her eyes were an amazingly deep blue. She was beautiful, not merely pretty, and there was in her eyes the haughty disdain of a queen who reprimands a clumsy subject.

"Pretty," he drawled slowly, "pretty, but plumb spoiled. Could be quite a lady, too," he added regretfully. Then he smiled and removed his hat. "Sorry, ma'am. If you'll let me know when you expect to use the street for a racetrack, I'll keep out of the way. I'll do my best to keep everybody else out of the way, too."

He turned as if to go, but her voice halted him.

"Wait!"

She took a couple of quick turns with the lines, jumped to the street, and marched up to him. Her eyes were arrogant and her nostrils tight with anger. "Did you mean to insinuate that I wasn't a lady?" she demanded. She held her horsewhip in her right hand, and he could see she intended to use it.

19

He smiled again. "I did," he said quietly. "You see, ma'am, it takes more than just beauty and a little money to make a lady. A lady is thoughtful of other people. A lady don't go racing around running people down with a buckboard, and, when she does come close, she comes back and apologizes."

Her eyes grew darker and darker and he could see the coldness of fury in them. "You," she snapped contemptuously, "a common cowpuncher, trying to tell me how to be a lady!"

She drew back the whip and struck furiously, but he was expecting it, and without even shifting his feet he threw up an arm and blocked the blow of the whip with his forearm. Then he dropped his hand over and grasped the whip. With a quick twist he jerked it from her hands.

The movement tilted her off balance and she fell forward into his arms. He caught her, looked down into her upturned face, into her eyes blazing with astonishment and frustrated anger, and at her parted lips. He smiled. "I'd kiss you," he drawled, "and you look invitin', and most like it would be a lot of fun, but I won't. You spirited kind kiss much better if you come and ask for it."

"Ask?" She tore herself free from him, trembling from head to foot. "I'd never kiss you if you were the last man alive."

"No, ma'am, I reckon not. You'd be standin' in line waitin', standin' away back."

A hard voice behind Lance stopped him short.

"Seems like you're takin' in a lot of territory around here, stranger. I'd like to ask you a few questions."

Lance turned slowly, careful to hold his hands away from his guns.

The thin-faced man was standing close by, his thumbs hooked in his belt. Two of the other men had spread out, one right and one left. The third man was out of sight, had circled behind him probably, or was across the buckboard from him.

"Let's have the questions," he replied calmly. "I'm right curious myself."

"I want to know," the man demanded, his eyes narrow and ugly, "where you was day before yesterday."

Lance was puzzled. "The day before yesterday? I was ridin' a good many miles from here. Why?"

"You got witnesses?" the thin man sneered. "You better have."

"What you gettin' at?" Lance demanded.

"I s'pose you claim you never heard of Joe Wilkins?"

Several men had gathered around now. Lance could hear them muttering among themselves at the mention of that name.

"What do you mean?" Lance asked. "Who is Joe Wilkins?"

"He was killed on Lost Creek trail the day before yesterday," the fellow snapped. "You was on that trail then, and there's them that think you done him in. You deny it?"

"Deny it?" Lance stared at the man, his eyes watchful. "Why, I never heard of Joe Wilkins, haven't any reason to kill him. 'Course, I haven't seen him."

"They found Wilkins," the thin man went on, his cruel eyes fastened on Lance, "drilled between the eyes. Shot with a six-gun. You was on that road, and he'd been carryin' money. You robbed him."

Lance watched the man steadily. There was something more behind this bald accusation than appeared on the surface. Either an effort was being made to force him to make a break so they could kill him, or the effort was to discredit him. If he made a flat denial, it would be considered that he was calling the fellow a liar, and probably would mean a shoot-out. Lance chuckled carelessly. "How'd you know I was on Lost Creek trail?"

"I seen you," the man declared.

"Then," Lance said gently, "you were on the trail, too. Or you were off it, because I didn't see you. If you were off the trail, you were hiding, and, if so, why? Did you kill this Wilkins?"

The man's eyes narrowed to slits, and suddenly Lance sensed a hint of panic in them. They had expected him to say something to invite a fight. Instead, he had turned the accusation on his accuser.

"No! I didn't kill him!" the man declared. "He was my friend!"

"Never noticed you bein' so friendly with him, Polti," a big farmer declared. "If you was, I don't think he knowed it."

"You shut up," Polti, the thin man, snapped, his eyes blazing. "I'll do the talkin' here."

"You talked enough," Lance replied calmly, "to make somebody right suspicious. Why are you so durned anxious to pin this killin' on a stranger?"

"You killed Wilkins," Polti growled harshly, and triumph shone in his eyes. "Somebody search his saddlebags! You all knew Wilkins had him some gold dust he used to carry around. I bet we'll find it."

"You seem right shore," Lance suggested. "Did you put it in my bag while I was in the Trail House? I saw you slippin' out."

"Tryin' to get out of it?" Polti sneered. "Well, you won't. I'm goin' to search them bags here and now."

Lance was very still, and his green eyes turned hard and cold. "No," he said flatly. "If anybody searches them bags, it won't be you, and it'll be done in the presence of witnesses."

"I'll search 'em!" Polti snapped. "Now!"

He wheeled, but before he could take even one step, Lance moved. He grabbed the thin man and spun him around. With a whining cry of fury, Polti went for his gun, but his hand never reached the holster. Lance's left hit Polti's chin with a crack like that of a blacksnake whip, and Polti sagged. A left and a right smashed him down, bleeding from the mouth.

"This don't look so good for you, stranger," the big farmer stated fearlessly. "Let's look at them bags."

"Right," Lance replied quietly. "An honest man ain't got anything to fear, they say, but it wouldn't surprise me none to find the dust there."

Watching him closely, the crowd, augmented now by a dozen more, followed him to his horse. Suddenly he stopped.

"No," he said, "a man might palm it if it's small." He turned to the girl who had driven the buckboard, and who now stood nearby. "Ma'am, my apologies for our earlier difficulty, and will you go through the bags for me?"

Her eyes snapped. "With pleasure! And hope I find the evidence!"

She removed the articles from the saddlebags one by one. They were few enough. Two boxes of .45 ammunition, one of rifle ammunition, some cleaning materials, and a few odds and ends of rawhide.

As she drew the packet of pictures out, one of them slipped from the packet and fell to the ground. The girl stopped quickly and retrieved it, glancing curiously at the picture of an elderly woman with a face of quiet dignity and poise. For an instant she glanced at Lance, then looked away.

"There is no gold here," she said quietly. "None at all."

"Well," Lance said, and turned, "I guess. . . ."

Polti was gone.

"Puts you in the clear, stranger," the big farmer said. "I wonder where it leaves Polti?"

"Mebbe he'd've tried to slip it into the saddlebag when he searched it," somebody suggested. "Wouldn't put it past him."

Lance glanced at the speaker. "That implies he has the gold dust. If he has, he probably killed Wilkins."

Nobody spoke, and Lance glanced from one to the other. A few men at the rear of the crowd began to sidle away. Finally the big farmer looked up.

"Well, nobody is goin' to say Jack Pickett lacks nerve," he

said, "but I ain't goin' to tackle Polti and them gun-slick *hombres* he trails with. It's like askin' for it."

The crowd dwindled, and Lance turned to find the golden-haired girl still standing there.

"I'm still not sure," she said coldly. "You could have buried it."

He grinned. "That's right, ma'am, I could have."

He turned and walked away. The girl stared after him, her brows knit.

Lance led the buckskin slowly down the street to the livery stable. He walked because he wanted to think, and he thought well on his feet. This thing had a lot of angles. Polti was mean and cruel. The man was obviously a killer who would stop at nothing. For some reason he had deliberately started out to frame Lance. Why, there seemed no reason. He might, of course, know why he had come to Live Oak and the town of Botalla.

In the livery stable Lance was rubbing down the buckskin when he heard a voice speak from the darkness of a stall behind him.

"Busy little feller, ain't you?"

The speaker stepped out of the stall into the light. He wore a battered hat, patched jeans, and a hickory shirt. Yet the guns on his hips looked business-like. Powerfully built, he had brick-red hair, and a glint of humor in his sardonic blue eyes.

"Name of Gates," he said. "They call me Rusty."

"I'm Lance."

The eyes of the stranger in Botalla took in the cowpuncher with quick intelligence. This man was rugged and capable. He looked as if he would do to ride the river with.

"So I heard." Rusty began making a smoke. Then he looked up, grinning. "Like I say, you're busy. You invite Steve Lord to a shootin' party, then side-step and let him off easy. A lot of people are askin' why. They want to know if you've throwed in with Chet Lord. They want to know if you was scared out. Then you tangle with that wildcat, Tana Steele. . . ."

"Webb Steele's daughter? I thought so. Noticed the name of Tana Steele on a package in the buckboard."

"Yeah. That's her, and trouble on wheels, pard. She'll never forgive, and, before she's through, she'll make you eat your words. She never quits."

"What do you know about this *hombre*, Polti?" asked Lance.

"Bert Polti? He's a sidewinder. Always has money, never does nothin'. He's plumb bad, an' plenty fast with that shootin' iron."

"He hangs out at the Spur?"

"Mostly. Him and them pards of his . . . Joe Daniels, Skimp Ellis, and Henry Bates. They're bad, all of them, and the bartender at the Spur is tough as a boot."

Lance started for the door. Rusty stared after him for an instant, then shrugged.

"Well," he said, "I'm buyin' a ticket. This is one ride I want to take." And he swung along after Lance.

Lance walked up on the boardwalk and shoved open the batwing doors of the Spur. Bert Polti had been looking for trouble, and now Lance was. Slow to anger, it mounted in him now like a tide, the memory of those small, vicious eyes and the tenseness of the man as he stood, set to make a kill.

Never a troublemaker, Lance had always resented being bullied, nevertheless, and he resented seeing others pushed around. It was this, as much as a debt to pay, that had brought him to Botalla. There was as yet no tangible clue to what the trouble here was all about. He had only Steve Lord's version, one that seemingly ignored the rights of Mort Davis. Yet now Polti was buying in. Polti had deliberately tried to frame him with a killing. Lance hadn't a doubt but that Polti had planned to plant gold dust in his saddlebags.

CHAPTER THREE

A half dozen men were loitering about the bar when Lance walked in, turned, and looked around.

"Where's Polti?" he demanded.

One of the men he had seen talking to Polti was sitting at a table nearby, another stood at the bar.

There was no reply. "I said," Lance repeated sharply, "where's Polti?"

"You won't find out nothin' here, stranger," the seated man drawled, his tone insulting. "When Polti wants you, he'll get you."

Lance took a quick step toward him and, catching a flicker of triumph in the man's eye, wheeled to see an upraised bottle aimed at his head. Before the man who held it could throw, Lance's gun fairly leaped from its holster. It roared and the shot caught the bottle just as it left the man's hand.

Liquor flew in all directions, and the man sprang back, splattered by it.

Holstering his gun, Lance stepped in and caught the man by the shirt and jerked him around. Instantly the fellow swung. Turning him loose, Lance hooked a short left to the chin, then stabbed two fast jabs to the face. He feinted, and threw a high hard right. The fellow went down and rolled over on the floor.

Without a second's warning, Lance whirled around and grabbed the wrist of the man at the chair, spun him around, and hurled him to the floor.

26

"All right!" he snapped. "Talk, or take a beatin'! Where's Polti?"

"The devil with you!" Lance's latest victim snarled. "I'll kill you!"

Then Lance had him off the floor, slammed him against the bar, and proceeded to slap and backhand him seven times so fast the eye could scarcely follow. His grip was like iron, and before that strength the man against the bar felt impotent and helpless.

"Talk, cuss you!" Lance barked, and slapped him again. The man's head bobbed with the force of the blow. "I'm not talkin' for fun!" Lance said. "I want an answer!"

"Apple Cañon," the man muttered surlily, "and I hope he kills you."

Lance slammed him to the floor alongside the first man, then spun on his heel, and walked out. As he came through the door, he saw Rusty Gates standing outside, hand on his gun. Gates grinned.

"Didn't take long," he said dryly. "You operate pretty fast, pardner."

"Where's Apple Cañon?" Lance demanded.

"Well," Gates said, and rolled his quid of chewing in his jaws, "Apple Cañon is almost due south of here, down close to the border. That's where Nita Riordan hangs out."

"Who's she?" Lance wanted to know.

"Queen of the Border, they call her. Half Irish, half Mexican, and all dynamite. The best-looking woman in the Southwest, and a tiger when she gets started. But it ain't her you want to watch. It's Brigo. Jaime Brigo is a big Yaqui half-breed who can sling a gun as fast as the Brockmans, track like a bloodhound, and is loyal as a Saint Bernard. Also, he weighs about two pounds less than a ton of coal."

"What's the place like . . . a town?"

"No. A bar, a bunkhouse, and three or four houses. It's a hang-out for outlaws. And, feller, it ain't no place for a man t' go lookin' for Bert Polti. That's his bailiwick."

Lance saddled Buck, his buckskin, and headed south, leaving Rusty at the stable, staring thoughtfully after him. The day was beginning to fade now, and he could see the sun grow larger as it slid away toward the western mountains. There was still heat. It would not be tempered until after the sun was gone, until the long shadows came to make the plains cool.

The bunch grass levels were dotted with mesquite and clumps of prickly pear, and Lance rode on through them, letting the buckskin have his head on the narrow winding trail. Prairie dog towns were all about, but they disappeared as the rocks grew closer. Once he saw a rattler, and there were always buzzards, circling on slow, majestic wings above the waste below.

When he had gone no more than two miles, he left the trail and started across country, still thinking of Polti. He did not trust this man. He began to dig and pry in his memory, trying to uncover some clue as to Polti's actions. But more and more it became apparent that the secret of all the trouble lay in something he did not know.

The dim trail he had taken when he left the main trail to Apple Cañon was lifting now, skirting the low hills, steadily winding higher and higher. The story that he was going to Apple Cañon was a good one. It would cover up what he actually intended to do. And soon he would go to Apple Cañon.

Polti was dangerous. He knew that. Nor did he underrate the two men he had beaten up in the Spur. Their kind were coyotes who would follow a man for months for a chance to pull him down.

There was menace in this country, an impending sense of danger that would not leave him. There was more here than met the eyes, more than the smile on tall, handsome Steve Lord's face, more than the sullen anger of the lovely, pampered Tana. There was death here, death and the acrid smell of gunpowder.

What did they know? What was behind the message he had received that had brought him here? Was it just another range war, or was it more?

Yet anyone who had lived in Texas through the Taylor and Sutton feud knew that range war could be deadly. And in Texas these days men rode with awareness. The wire was stirring up old feelings, old animosities. The big ranches were all stringing wire now. The smaller ranches were doing likewise. Starved for range for their herds, and pinched down to small areas, they saw extinction facing them if they did not fight. And they had neither the wealth to hire gunmen, nor the strength to fight without them unless they banded together.

Joe Wilkins, who Lance had learned was a nester, had been slain. The mention of his name and the quick surge of feeling had been enough to indicate that submerged fires burned here, and close to the surface. Any little spark might touch off an explosion that would light a thousand fires along the border, and turn it into an inferno of gunsmoke. Men were all carrying guns. They were carrying spare ammunition, too. They were ready, one and all. They rode the range, or rode fence with rifles across their saddle bows, and their keen eyes searched every clump of mesquite or prickly pear. Joe Wilkins had died, fences had been cut, and the ugly shape of war was lifting its head.

It was a time when men shot first and asked questions afterward. The notorious outlaw, Sam Bass, was riding the trails, robbing banks and trains. John Wesley Hardin was running up his score of twenty-seven men killed. King Fisher had five hundred men riding to his orders on both sides of the border, King Fisher with his tiger-skin chaps and silver-loaded sombrero. Wild Bill Hickok, Bat Masterson, Billy Tilghman, Ben Thompson, and a hundred other gun slicks and toughs were riding the trails, acting as marshals in towns, or gambling.

The long fences were cutting down the range. The big ranches would still have range, but there would be too little grass for the cattle of the small ranchers. For them it was the end, or a battle for survival, and such a battle could have but one result. Yet the small ranchers were banding together. They were wearing guns.

From the crest of a ridge, Lance looked over the valley of Lost Creek and could see the long silvery strands of barbed wire stretching away as far as the eye could reach.

"I don't know, about this wire business," he mused, patting the buckskin on the shoulder. "I don't know who's right. There's arguments for both sides. It gives everybody a chance to improve breedin' and have crops, and anybody can see the longhorn is on the way out. Too little beef. These whitefaces now, they have something. They carry a lot more beef than a longhorn. You and me, Buck, mebbe we're on the way out, too. We're free, and we go where we please, and we don't like fences. If they build fences, this country is finished for us. We'll have to go to Dakota, or mebbe to Mexico or the Argentine."

The buckskin turned down the little trail through the tumbled boulders and cedar, a dim, concealed little trail that the sure-footed mountain horse followed even in the vague light of late evening. This was not an honest man's trail, but Lance was not worried for he knew the manner of man he rode to see. That man who would never be less than honest, but he would fight to the last ditch for what he believed to be his own.

The trail dipped into a hollow several hundred yards across, and, when Lance had ridden halfway across it, he dismounted and led his horse into a sheltered position behind a boulder. It would be a long wait, for he was early. Sitting against a boulder, he watched the declining sun fall slowly westward, watched the shadows creep up the rocky walls, and the sunlight splash color upon the cliffs.

He must have fallen asleep, for when he awakened the stars were out, and he judged several hours must have passed.

It was quiet, yet when Lance lifted his eyes, it was in time to catch the gleam of starlight on a pistol barrel aimed over a rock. Then, even as he moved, the muzzle flowered with flame. As he hurled himself desperately to one side, he heard the bullet strike, then again, and something struck him a wicked blow on the back of the head. He tumbled on his face among the boulders. In his fading consciousness he seemed to feel something hot and sticky along his cheek. . . .

The first thing Lance knew, a long time later, was the throbbing pain in his skull as though a thousand tiny iron men were hammering with red-hot hammers at the shell of his skull, pounding and pounding. He opened his eyes to see a distant star shining through a crevice in the rocks across the hollow. Then he saw something, long and dark, lying upon the ground. It was like the body of a man.

Turning over painfully, Lance got his hands under him and pushed himself up to his knees. For a long time then he was still, and his head swayed and seemed like an enormous, uncontrollable thing. He forced his eyes to focus, but the starlight was too slight to help him to see more than he had.

Then he got a hand on the rock beside him, and pushed himself to his feet. There he remained, leaning against the rock. One hand dropped instinctively to his gun on the right side, then he felt for the other. Both were there.

The first shot, if there had been more than one, had missed him. It had either ricocheted off a rock then and hit him, or else the unseen killer had fired again. He apparently had been left for dead. Feeling of his skull, he could understand why, for his hair was matted with blood.

Feeling around, his head throbbing fiercely, he found his hat and hung it around his neck by the rawhide chin strap. His head was too swollen for him to wear the sombrero. Stumbling to where he had left his horse, he found Buck waiting patiently. The yellow horse pricked up his ears and whinnied softly.

"Sorry, Buck," Lance whispered. "You should've been in the stable by now, with a good bait of oats."

He had swung into the saddle and turned down into the hollow before he remembered the shape on the ground. Then he saw it again.

There was more than the shape, for there was a standing horse. He dismounted and, gun in hand, walked cautiously over to the body. It was that of a stranger. In the vague starlight he could see only the outline of the man's features, but it was no one he knew. Then he saw the white of the envelope.

Stooping, his head pounding, he picked it up. There was writing on the back. By the light of a shielded match, he read a painful scrawl:

Mort needs help bad. I wuz dry gulched. He koodnt kum.

It was written on the back of a letter addressed to **Sam Carter, Lost Creek Ranch.** Scratched by a dying man.

Thrusting the letter into his pocket, Lance wheeled his horse and rode away down the trail.

Lost Creek Ranch lay ahead and to the south, but he turned the buckskin again and rode away from the trail, skirting a cluster of rocks and heading for the ranch, whose position he had ascertained from Rusty, and knew from a map that had been sent him. He drew his rifle from its boot and put it across his saddle bow.

Still several miles away, he saw a glow in the sky. A glow of burning buildings. His eyes grew hard, and he spoke urgently to Buck. The long-eared yellow horse quickened his pace.

Lance passed what must have been Mort Davis's fence, but

some of the posts were down, and the wire was gone. Lance refrained from watching the fire, keeping his eyes on the surrounding darkness. Maybe he was too late. A house was burning, and perhaps Mort Davis was dead. Suddenly he saw a man ride out of the shadows.

"That you, Joe?" the man shouted.

Lance reined in, and swung his horse on an angle to the man. The fellow came closer.

"What's the matter?" he demanded. "Can't you hear me?"

The speaker was one of the two men Lance had whipped in the bar earlier that day. They recognized each other at the same instant. With a startled gasp the fellow went for his gun. Lance pulled the trigger without shifting the rifle, and the man grabbed his stomach, sliding from the saddle with a groan.

CHAPTER FOUR

Without looking down, Lance started toward the glow of the fire, his face set and angry. Had they killed Mort?

They had not. Lance was still several hundred yards away when he saw a rifle flash and heard the heavy bark of Mort's old Sharps. Several shots replied.

Touching spurs to the buckskin, Lance whipped into the circle near the flames at a dead run, snapping three quick shots into a group of men near a low adobe wall. It was a gamble at that speed, but the attacking group was bunched close. There was a cry of pain, and one of them whirled about. He was fully in the light and his chest loomed up. Lance put a shot into him as he flashed abreast of the man, heard a bullet whip past his own ear. Then he was gone into the darkness beyond the light of the flames.

Sliding from saddle, Lance put the rifle to his shoulder and shot twice. Reloading in haste, he began smoking up every bit of cover near the burning house, taking targets when they offered, and seeking the darkest spots of cover at other times. When his rifle was emptied, he dropped it to his side and opened up with a six-gun.

Men broke from cover and ran for their horses. The old Sharps bellowed in protest at their escape, and one of the men fell headlong. He scrambled up, but made only three steps before he pitched over again, dangerously near the flames.

Again Lance reloaded, then walked forward.

"Mort!" he called. "Come out of there, you old wolf! I know your shootin'!"

A tall, dark-bearded man in a battered black felt hat sauntered down from the circle of rocks at the foot of the cliff.

"Looks like you got here just in time, friend," he said. "You see Sam?"

Briefly Lance explained. Then he jerked his head in the direction the attackers had taken. "Who were they?" he asked.

"I don't know. Mebbe Webb Steele's boys. Him and Lord want me out of here, the worst way." He scratched the stubble on his lean jaws. "Let's have us a look."

Three men had been left behind. With the man Lance had killed out on the prairie, that made four. It had been a costly lesson. Well, Lance told himself, they should have known better than to tackle an old he-wolf like Mort Davis.

A lean, gangling sixteen-year-old strolled down from the rocks. He carried a duplicate of his father's Sharps. He stood beside his father and stared at the bodies.

"Don't look like nobody I ever seen," Mort said thoughtfully, "but Webb and Chet both been a-gettin' in some new hands."

"Pap," the youngster said, "I seen this one in Botalla trailin' with Bert Polti."

Lance studied the man's face. It wasn't one of the men he knew. "Mort," he asked, "where do the Brockmans figger in this?"

The old man puckered his brow. "The Brockmans? I didn't know they was in it. Abel Brockman rode for Steele once, but not no more. He got to sparkin' Tana, and the old man let him go. He didn't like it none, neither."

"It don't look right," Lance said as he rubbed his jaw reflectively. "Lord and Steele are supposed t' be fightin', but so far all I've seen is this gang that trails with Polti. They jumped me in town."

"Watch them Brockmans," Mort said seriously. "They're poison mean, and they never fight alone. Always the two of 'em together, and they got this gunfightin' as a team worked out mighty smooth. They always get you in a spot where you can't get the two at once."

Lance looked around. "Burned all your buildin's, didn't they? Any place you can live?"

"Uhn-huh. We got us a little cave back up here. We lived there before we built us a house. We'll make out. We're used to gettin' along without much. This here's the best place we had for a long time if we can keep it."

"You'll keep it," Lance promised, his face harsh and cold.

Mort Davis had done his share in making the West a place to live. He was getting old now, and deserved the rewards of his work. No big outfit, or outlaws either, was going to drive him off, if Lance could help it.

"Who knew this Sam Carter was to meet me?" he asked. "Or that you were?"

"Nobody I know of," said old Mort. "Carter's a 'puncher who started him a little herd over back of the butte. We worked together some. He was settin' for chuck when them riders come down on us. I asked him to get you."

Lance sketched the trouble in Botalla, then added the account of his run-in with Tana Steele. Mort grinned at that.

"I'd 'a' give a purty to seen that," he said. "Tana's had her head for a long time. Drives that there buckboard like a crazy woman! At that, she can ride nigh anythin' that wears hair, and she will! Best-lookin' woman around here, too, unless it's Nita Riordan."

"The woman at Apple Cañon?" Lance asked quickly.

"Yep. All woman, too. Runs that shebang by herself. Almost, that is. Got her a Yaqui half-breed to help. Ain't nobody to fool with, that Injun."

"You better hole up and stay close to home, Mort," Lance said after a minute. "I'm dead tired, but I've some ridin' to do. I caught a couple of hours' sleep back in the hollow before the trouble."

He swung into saddle and started back over the trail. It was late and he was tired, but he needed more information before he could even start to figure things out. One thing he knew. He must talk to Lord and Steele and try to stop the trouble until they could get together. And he must get more information.

Four of the enemy had died, but, even as he told himself that, he remembered that none of the dead men had been in any sense a key man. They were just straw men, men who carried guns and worked for hire, and more could be found to fill their places.

And then Sam Carter was gone. A good man, Sam. A man who could punch cows, and who had enough stuff in him to start his own place, and to fight for what he knew was right. No country could afford to lose men like that.

Suddenly, on the inspiration of the moment, Lance whirled the buckskin from the trail and headed for the Webb Steele spread. He could try talking to Steele, anyway.

He was well into the yard before a man stepped from the shadows.

"All right, stranger! Keep your hands steady. Now light, easy-like, and walk over here."

Lance obeyed without hesitation, carefully keeping his hands in front of him in the light from the ranch house window. A big man stepped from the shadows and walked up to him. Instinctively Lance liked the hard, rugged face of the other man.

"Who are you?" the man demanded.

"Name of Lance. Ridin' by and thought I'd drop in and have a talk with Webb Steele."

"Lance?" Something sparked in the man's eyes. "You the

gent had the run-in with Miss Tana?"

"That's me. She still sore?"

"Lance"—the older man chuckled—"shore as I'm Jim Weston, you've let yourself in for a packet of trouble. That gal never forgets! When she come in this afternoon, she was fit to be tied!" He holstered his gun. "What you aimin' to see Webb about?"

"Stoppin' this war. Ain't no sense to it."

"What's your dicker in this?" Weston asked shrewdly. "Man don't do nothin' unless he's got a angle somewheres."

"What's your job here, Weston?" Lance said.

"Foreman," Weston announced. "Why?"

"Well, what's the ranch makin' out of this war? What are you makin'?"

"Not a cussed thing, cowboy. She's keepin' me up nights, and we got all our 'punchers guardin' fence when they should be tendin' to cows. We're losin' cattle, losin' time, losin' wire, and losin' money."

"Shore. Well, you don't like that. I don't like it, either. But my own angle is Mort Davis. Mort's a friend of mine, and, Weston, Mort's goin' to keep his place in Lost Creek. He'll keep it, or, by glory, there'll be Lord and Steele 'punchers planted under every foot of it."

"Think you're pretty salty, don't you?" Weston demanded, but there was a glint of understanding in his eye. "Well, mebbe you are."

"I've been around, Weston. But that don't matter. You and me can talk. You're an old trail hand yourself. You're a buffalo hunter, too. What you got against Mort?"

"Nothin'. He's a sight better hand and a whole lot better man than lots of 'em ridin' for this ranch now." He shook his head. "I know what you mean, mister. I know exactly. But I don't make the rules for the ranch. Webb does . . . Webb, or Tana."

They stepped inside the ranch house, and Weston tapped on an inner door. At a summons, he opened it. Big Webb Steele was tipped back in his chair across the table from the door. His shirt was open two buttons, showing a hairy chest, and his hard level eyes seemed to stare through and through Lance. To his right was Tana, and, as she saw Lance, she came to her feet instantly, her eyes blazing. Across the table was a tall, handsome man in a plain black suit of fine cut, a man with blue-gray eyes and a small, neatly trimmed blond mustache.

"You!" Tana burst out. "You have the nerve to come out here?"

"I reckon, ma'am," Lance drawled, and he smiled slyly. "I didn't reckon you carried your whip in the house. Or do you carry it everywhere?"

"You take a high hand with my daughter, Lance, if that's your name," Webb rumbled, glancing from Tana to Lance and back. "What happened between you two?"

"Steele," Lance said, grinning a little, "your daughter was drivin' plumb reckless, and we had a few words in which I attempted to explain that the roads wasn't all built for her own pleasure."

Webb chuckled. "Young feller, you got a nerve. But Tana can fight her own battles, so heaven have mercy on your soul."

"Well," Lance said, "you spoke of me takin' a high hand with your daughter. If my hand had been applied where it should have been, it might've done a lot more good."

Webb grinned again, and his hard eyes twinkled. "Son, I'd give a hundred head of cows to see the man as could do that. It'd be right interestin'."

"Father!" Tana protested. "This man insulted me."

"Ma'am," Lance interrupted, "I'd shore admire to continue

this argument some other time. Right now I've come to see Mister Steele on business."

"What business?" Webb Steele demanded, cutting short Tana's impending outburst.

"War business. You're edgin' into a three-cornered war that's goin' to cost you plenty. It's goin' to cost Chet Lord plenty, too. I come to see about stoppin' it. I want to get a peace talk between you an' Chet Lord an' Mort Davis."

"Mort Davis?" Webb exploded. "That no-account nester ain't goin' to make no peace talk with me! He'll get off that claim or we'll run him off!" Webb's eyes were blazing. "You tell that long-eared highbinder to take his stock and get!"

"He's caused a lot of trouble here," the man with the blond mustache said, "cutting fences and the like. He's a menace to the range." He looked up at Lance. "I'm Victor Bonham," he added. "Out from New York."

Lance had seated himself, and he studied Bonham for an instant, then looked back at Webb Steele, ignoring the Eastern man.

"Mister Steele," he said, "you've got the rep of bein' a square shooter. You come West with some durned good men, some of the real salty ones. Well, so did Mort Davis. Mort went farther West than you. He went on to Santa Fe and to Salt Lake. He helped open this country up. Then he finds him a piece of ground and settles down. What's so wrong about that?" Lance shifted his chair a little, then went on. "He fought Comanches and Apaches. He built him a place. He cleaned up that water hole. He did things in Lost Creek you'd never have done. You'd never have bothered about it but for this fencin' business. Well, Mort Davis moved in on that place, and he's a-goin' to stay. I, for one, mean to see he stays." He leaned forward. "Webb Steele, I ain't been hereabouts long, but I been here long enough to know something mighty funny is goin' on. Mort Davis was burned out tonight, by somebody's orders, an' I don't think the orders were yours or Chet Lord's, either. Well, as I said, Mort stays right where he is, and, if he dies, I'm goin' to move in an' bring war to these hills like nobody ever saw before."

"You talk mighty big for a loose-footed cowhand," Bonham said, smiling coldly. "We might decide not to let you leave here at all."

Lance turned his head slowly at the direct challenge and for a long minute he said nothing, letting his chill green eyes burn into the Easterner. "I don't know what your stake is in this, Bonham," he said evenly, "but when I want to leave here, I'm goin' to. I'll leave under my own power, and, if I have to walk over somebody in gettin' out, I could start with you."

"Better leave him alone, Bonham," a new voice interrupted. "He means what he says."

They all looked up, startled. Rusty Gates stood in the doorway, a sardonic smile on his hard red face.

"I was ridin' by," he explained, "and thought I'd rustle some coffee. But take a friendly tip."

Bonham laughed harshly. "I. . . ."

"Better shut up, New York man," Gates said. "There's been enough killin' tonight. You keep talkin', you're goin' to say the wrong thing." Rusty smiled suddenly, and glanced at Lance, his eyes twinkling. "Y' see"—he lit his smoke—"I've heard Lance Kilkenny was right touchy about what folks said of him."

CHAPTER FIVE

The name dropped into the room like a bombshell. Tana's hands went to her throat, and her eyes widened. Webb Steele dropped his big hands to the table and his chair legs slammed down. Jim Weston backed up a little, his tongue wetting his lips.

It was Bonham, the man from New York, who Lance Kilkenny was watching, and in Bonham's eyes he saw a sudden blaze of white, killing rage. The man's lips drew back in a thin line. If ever lust to kill was in a man's face, it was in Victor Bonham's then. An instant only, and then it was gone so suddenly that Kilkenny wondered if it had not been a hallucination.

"Did you say . . . Kilkenny?" Webb Steele demanded. "The gunfighter?"

"That's right." Lance's voice seemed to have changed suddenly. "My name is Lance Kilkenny. Mort Davis was in trouble, so I came to help him." He glanced at Webb. "I don't want trouble, if I can avoid it, but they tried to burn out Mort and wipe him out."

"What happened?" Bonham demanded.

"Four men died," Lance said quietly. "They were not men anybody ever saw ridin' with Steele or Lord." He smiled a little. "Mort's still around, and still able."

Bonham was staring at him. "Yes, I seem to recall something about a man named Kilkenny being nursed by Davis, after a fight."

Lance got up. "Think it over, Mister Steele. I'm not ridin' for war. I never asked for trouble with any man. But Mort's my friend. Even with two old prairie wolves like you and Chet Lord there can be peace. You two should get together with Mort. You'd probably like each other."

Kilkenny stepped backward out of the door and went down the steps to the buckskin. Tana Steele stood there beside the horse. He had seen her slip from the room an instant before he left.

"So," she said, scorn in her voice, "you're a gunman. I might have known it. A man who shoots down other men, less skilled than he, then holds himself up as a dangerous man."

"Ma'am," Kilkenny said quietly, taking the bridle, "I've killed men. Most of 'em needed it, all of 'em asked for it. What you say doesn't help any, or make it worse." He swung into the saddle. "Ma'am," he added softly, "you're shore pretty in the moonlight . . . where a body can't see the meanness in you. You've either got an awful streak somewhere to make you come out here and say somethin' unpleasant, or else"—he grinned impudently—"you're fallin' in love with me."

Tana started back angrily. "In love with you? Why . . . why, you conceited, contemptible. . . ."

But the buckskin swung around and Lance dropped an arm about her waist and swung her from the ground. He was laughing, and then he kissed her. He held her and kissed her until her lips responded almost in spite of themselves. Then he put her down and swung out of the ranch yard at a gallop, lifting his voice in song.

> *Old Joe Clark has got a cow*
> *She was muley born.*
> *It takes a jaybird forty-eight hours*
> *To fly from horn to horn.*

Tana Steele, shaking with anger or some other emotion less easily understood, stood staring after him. She was still staring when his voice died away in the distance.

Then she heard another horse start up, and watched it gallop down the trail after Lance Kilkenny.

It was several minutes before the rider caught up with Kilkenny, and found him, gun in hand, facing downtrail from the shadows at the edge. It was Rusty Gates. "What do you want?" Kilkenny demanded.

Rusty leaned forward and patted his black on the neck.

"Why, I reckon I want to ride along with you, Kilkenny. I hear you're a straight shooter, and I guess you're the only *hombre* I ever met up with could get into more trouble than me. If you can use a man to side you, I'd shore admire to ride along. I got an idea," he added, "that in days to come you can use some help."

"Let's ride, Rusty," Kilkenny said quietly. "It's getting' late. . . ."

When Lance Kilkenny rolled out of his blankets in the early dawn, he glanced over at Gates. The redhead was still snoring. Kilkenny grinned, then shook his boots carefully to clear out any wandering tarantulas or scorpions that might have holed up for the night. Grimly he contemplated a hole in his sock. No time for that now. He pulled the sock down to cover the exposed toe, and slid the boot on. Then he got up. Carefully he checked his guns.

He moved quietly out of camp. For ten minutes he made a painstaking search of the area. When he returned to camp, he saddled his horse and rode quietly away. He was back, and had bacon frying when Rusty awakened and sat up.

They had camped on a cedar-covered mountainside with a wide view of Lost Creek Valley. From the ridge above they could see away into the purple distance of the mountains of Mexico. The air was brisk and cool with morning.

Coffee was bubbling in the pot when Rusty walked over.

"You get around, pardner," he said. "Shore, I slept like a log. Hey!" He looked startled and pleased. "You got bacon!"

"Got it last night from that Mexican where we got the *frijoles*. He's got him a half dozen hogs."

Rusty shook himself, and grinned. Then he looked up, suddenly serious.

"Ever see this *hombre* Bonham before?" he asked.

"No." Kilkenny glanced sideward at Gates. "Know him?"

"No. He ain't from around here."

"I wonder."

"You wonder? Why? They said he was from New York. He looks like a pilgrim."

"Yeah, he does." Lance poured coffee into two cups. "But he knew about Mort carin' for me after the fight with the Webers."

"Heard it around probably. I heard that myself." Rusty grinned. "You're too suspicious."

"I'm still alive." Lance Kilkenny grinned wryly.

Rusty nodded. "You got something there. Don't pay to miss no bets. Who you think Bonham is?"

Lance shrugged. "No idea."

"You had an idea last night. You said this fightin' wasn't all Lord an' Steele."

"You think it is?" asked Kilkenny.

Rusty shook his head. "No. Can't be. But who?"

"You been here longer than I have. How does she stack up to you? Who stands to gain but Steele and Lord? Who stands to gain if they both get gunned out or crippled?"

"Nobody. Them two have got it all, everywheres around here. Except for Mort, of course, but Mort ain't grabby. He wants his chunk of Lost Creek Valley, that's all."

45

"Rusty, you ever see a map of this country?"

"Map? Shucks, no! Don't reckon there is one. Who'd want a map?"

"Maps are handy things," Kilkenny said, sipping his coffee. "Sometimes a country looks a sight different on a map than you think it does. Sometimes, when you get a bird's eye view of things, you get a lot of ideas. Look here."

Drawing with his finger in the sand, Lance Kilkenny drew a roughly shaped V showing the low mountains and hills that girded the Live Oak country. Off to one side he drew in Lost Creek Valley.

"Right here, where it opens on the main valley," he said, "is where Lord and Steele's fence lines come together."

"That's right, plumb right," Rusty agreed. "That's what all the fuss is about. Who gets the valley?"

"But notice," Lance said, "this V-shaped valley that is half Steele's and half Lord's runs from the point of the V up to the wide cattle ranges of Texas. And up there are other cow outfits, bigger than even Lord's and Steele's. Fine stock, too. I come down through there a while back and rode over some fine range. Lots of whiteface bulls brought in up there. The stock is bein' improved. In a few years this is goin' to be one of the greatest stock-raisin' countries in the world. The fences won't make much difference at first except to limit the size of the roundups. There won't be no more four county roundups, but the stock will all improve, more beef per steer, and a bigger demand for it. The small ranchers can't afford to get good bulls. They'll cut fences here and there, as much to let bulls in with their old stock as anything. But that's only part of it. Look at all these broad miles of range. They'll be covered with fat stock, thousands upon thousands of head. It'll be fat stock, good grass, and plenty of water. They'll shift the herds and feed the range off little by little. You've punched cows long enough to have

46

rustled a few head. Huh, we all have now and again. Just think now, all this is stock country up here above the V. Now foller my finger." He drew a trail in the dust down through the point of the V into the country below. "See?" he asked.

Rusty furrowed his brow and spoke thoughtfully. "You mean somebody could rustle that stock into Mexico? Shore, but they'd have to drive rustled cows across the Steele and the Lord spreads, and. . . ." His eyes narrowed suddenly. "Say, pardner, I get it. You mean, if Lord and Steele was both out of it, whoever controlled that V could do as he danged well pleased down there. Right?"

Kilkenny nodded. "What's this place at the point of the V?"

"That's Apple Cañon. It's the key to the whole country, ain't it? And it's a hang-out for outlaws!"

"Shore, Apple Cañon. The Live Oak country is like a big funnel that will pour rustled stock down into Mexico, and whoever controls the Live Oak and Apple Cañon controls rustlin' in all this section of Texas!"

"Well, I'll be durned!" Rusty spat into the dust. "And that's where Nita Riordan lives!"

Kilkenny got up. "That's right, Rusty. Right as rain, and we're ridin' to have a little talk with Nita. We're ridin' now."

Llano Trail lifted up over the low hills from the Live Oak country and headed down again through Forgotten Pass, winding leisurely across the cactus-studded desert where only the coyotes prowled and rattlesnakes huddled in the shade of boulders, and the chaparral cock ran along the dim trails. Ahead of the two horsemen, lost like motes in a beam in all the vast emptiness of the desert, could be seen the great, ragged rocks of the mountains. Not mountains of great height, but huge, upthrust masses of rock, weirdly shaped as though wrought by some insane god.

Louis L'Amour

It was a country almost without water, yet a country where a knowing man might live, for barrel cactus, the desert reservoir, grew there. One might cut a hole in the cactus and during the night or in a matter of an hour or so considerable liquid, cool and fresh, would gather. Always sufficient for life.

The buckskin ambled easily, accustomed to long trails, and accustomed to having his head in pacing over the great distances. His was a long-stepping, untiring walk that ate up the miles.

The sun lifted from behind a morning cloud, and started climbing toward noon. Buzzards wheeled lazily, their far-seeing eyes searching the desert in an endless quest for food.

Slouching in his saddle, his hard face burned almost as red as his hair, Rusty Gates watched the rider ahead of him. It was easy to admire a fighting man, he thought. Always a fighter himself, Rusty fought because it was easy for him, because it was natural. He had punched cows, ridden the cattle trails north. He had, one time and another, tried everything, been everywhere a man could go on a horse. Usually he rode alone. But slowly and surely down the years he began picking up lore on Lance Kilkenny. He had it at his fingertips now.

CHAPTER SIX

Everyone, Rusty Gates thought, knew about Hickok; everyone knew about John Wesley Hardin, and about Ben Thompson and his partner, Phil Coe. Not many knew about Kilkenny. He was a man who always moved on. He stayed nowhere long enough to build a solid reputation. Always it seemed, he had just gone. There was something so elusive about him, he had come to seem almost a phantom. Someone picked trouble with him, someone was killed, and Kilkenny was gone. Once they tried to rob him in a gambling den in Abilene. Two men had died. Apaches had cornered him in a ruined house in New Mexico, and, when the Apaches had drawn off, they had left seven dead behind them. In a hand-to-hand fight in Trail City he had whipped three men with fists and chairs. Then, when morning came, he was gone.

The stories of the number of men he had killed varied. Some said he had killed eighteen men, not counting Indians and Mexicans. The cattle buyer back in Dodge, who had made a study of such things, said he had killed not less than twenty-nine. Of this Kilkenny said nothing, and no man could find him to put the question.

"You know," Rusty said suddenly, breaking in on his own thoughts of Kilkenny, "the Brockmans hang out in Apple Cañon."

"Yeah." Kilkenny sat sideward in the saddle, to rest. "I know. We might run into 'em."

"Well," Rusty said, and he rolled the chew of tobacco in his jaws and spat, "there's better places to meet 'em than Apple Cañon. There'll be fifty men there, mebbe a hundred, and all friends of the Brockmans."

Kilkenny nodded and rolled a smoke. Then he grinned whimsically. "What you worried about?" he asked. "You got fifty rounds, ain't you?"

"Fifty rounds?" Gates exclaimed. "Shore, but shucks, man, I miss once in a while." He looked at Kilkenny speculatively. "You seen the Brockmans? They'll weigh about forty pounds more'n you, and you must weigh two hundred. I seen Cain Brockman shoot a crow on the wing!"

"Did the crow have a gun?" drawled Kilkenny.

That, decided Rusty, was a good question. It was one thing to shoot at a target even such a fleeting one as a bird on the wing. It was quite something else when you had to shoot at a man with a flaming gun in his fist. Yes, it made a sight of difference.

"By the way"—Kilkenny turned back in his saddle—"I want the Brockmans myself."

"Both of 'em?" Rusty was incredulous. "Listen, I. . . ."

"Both of 'em," Kilkenny said positively. "You keep the sidewinders off my back."

Rusty glanced up and saw a distant horseman coming toward them at an easy lope. He was still some distance away.

"Somebody comin'," he told Kilkenny. "One man."

"It's Steve Lord," Kilkenny said. "I picked him up a couple of miles back."

"Don't tell me you can see his face from here!" Rusty protested. "Why I can barely see it's a man!"

"Uhn-huh." Kilkenny grinned. "Look close. See the sunlight glintin' on that sombrero? Steve has a hatband made of polished silver disks. Not common."

Rusty spat. Easy enough when you figure it out, he thought, but not many would think of it. Now that it was mentioned he recalled that hatband. He had seen it so many times it no longer made an impression.

Suddenly he asked Kilkenny: "About that Mendoza deal. I was in Sonora after you killed him. I heard he was the fastest man in the world with a gun, then you beat him to it. Did you get the jump or was you just naturally faster?"

Kilkenny shrugged. "Didn't amount to much. He beat me to the draw, though."

"I didn't think anybody ever beat you," observed Rusty.

"He did. Mebbe he saw me a split second sooner. Fact, I think he did."

"How come he didn't kill you?" Rusty glanced at him curiously.

"He made a mistake." Kilkenny wiped sweat from Buck's neck. "He missed his first shot. Never," he added dryly, "miss the first one. You may not get another."

Steve Lord came up at a gallop and reined in sharply. "You!" he said, as he glanced sharply from one to the other. "Didn't know you was interested down thisaway."

"Takin' a look at Apple Cañon," Rusty said. He grinned widely. "I'm a-goin' to interduce Kilkenny to Nita."

"I heard you was Kilkenny," Steve said, and looked at him curiously. "I've talked to five men before who claimed to know you. Each gave a different description."

"Steve," Lance said, "this fight ain't goin' to do you or your old man any good. I had a talk with Webb Steele. I think we need a meetin' between your dad, Webb Steele, and Mort Davis to iron this trouble out."

"Mort Davis?" Steve exploded. "Why, Dad's threatened to shoot him on sight. They'd never dare get in the same room."

"I'll be there," Kilkenny said dryly. "If any shootin's done, I'll do it."

Steve shook his head doubtfully. "I'll talk to him, but it won't do any good. He's too hard-headed."

"So's Webb Steele," Rusty agreed, "but we'll bring him around."

"No need for anybody to fight," Kilkenny said. "I came in this to help Mort. You and your dad stand to lose plenty if this war breaks wide open. Why fight when it's to somebody else's interest?"

Steve's head jerked around. "What you mean by that?" he demanded.

Kilkenny looked up mildly, then drew deeply on his cigarette, and flicked off the ash before he replied. "Because there's somebody else in this," he said then. "Somebody who wants Lord and Steele out of the way, somebody who stands to win a heap. Find out who that is, and we'll know the reason for range war."

Steve's face sharpened. He wheeled his horse. "You won't find anybody at Apple Cañon!" he shouted. "I saw the Brockmans there!" Then he was gone.

"Scared," Rusty Gates suggested. "Scared silly."

"No," Kilkenny said, "he ain't scared. It's somethin' else."

Yet, as he rode on, he was not thinking of that, or of anything that had to do with this trouble except in the most remote way. He was thinking of himself, something he rarely allowed himself to do beyond caring for the few essential comforts of living, the obtaining of food and shelter. He was thinking of what lay ahead, for in his own mind he could see it all with bitter clarity.

This was an old story, and a familiar one. The West knew it, and would know it again and again in the bitter years to come. Struggle was the law of growth, and the West was growing up the hard way. It was growing up through a fog of gunsmoke, and through the acrid odor of gunpowder, and the sickly sweet smell of blood. Men would die, good men and bad, but strong men all, and a country needed its strong men. Such a country as this needed them doubly bad. Whether it would be today he did not know, but he knew there must be a six-gun showdown, and he had seen too many of them. He was tired. Young in years, he had ridden long on the out trail, and knew only too well what this meant. If he should be the best man, he would live to run again and to drift to a new land where he was not known as a killer, as a gunman. For a few days, a few months all would go well. Then there would come a time, as it was coming now, when it was freedom and right, or a fight to the death. Sometimes he wondered if it were worth it.

There was something familiar about this ride. He remembered it all so well. Ahead of him lay trouble, and going to Apple Cañon was typical of him, just what he would do. It was always his method to go right to the heart of trouble, and Apple Cañon seemed to be the key point here.

There was so much ahead. He did not underrate Bert Polti. The snake-eyed gunman was dangerous, quick as a cat, and vicious as a weasel. The man would kill and kill until he was finally put down full of lead. He would not quit, for there wasn't a yellow thing about the man. He would kill from ambush, yes. He would take every advantage, for he did not kill from bravado or for a reputation. He killed to gain his own ends, and for that reason there would be no limit to his killing. Yet at best Polti was a tool. A keen-edged tool, but a tool nevertheless. He was a gunman, ready to be used by a keener brain, and such a brain was using him now. Who it was, Kilkenny could not guess. Somehow he could not convince himself that behind the bluff boldness of Webb Steele lived the ice-cold mind of a killer. Nor from what he could discover was Chet Lord different.

No, the unknown man was someone else, someone beyond

the pale of the known, someone relentless and ruthless, someone with intelligence, skill, and command of men. And afterward there would be only the scant food, the harsh living of the fugitive, then again a new attempt to find peace in new surroundings. Someday he might succeed, but in his heart he doubted it.

He was in danger. The thought impressed him little, for he had always been in danger. The man he sought this time would be aware by now that he knew the danger lay not in Steele or Lord, but outside of them. Yet his very action in telling them what he thought might force the unknown into the open. And that was what he must do. He must force the play until at every move it brought the unknown more and more into the open until he was compelled to reveal himself.

The direct attack. It was always best with the adroit man. Such a man could plan for almost anything but continuous frontal attack. And he, Kilkenny, had broken such plots before. But could he break this one? Looking over the field, he realized suddenly that he was not sure. This man was cool, deadly, and dangerous. He would anticipate Kilkenny's moves, and from the shelter of his ghost-like existence he could hunt him, pin him down, and kill him—if he was lucky.

Kilkenny looked curiously at the mountains ahead. Somewhere up there Forgotten Pass went over the mountains and then down to the Río Grande. It wasn't much of a pass, as passes go, and the section was barren, remote. But it would undoubtedly be an easy route over which to take cattle to Mexico, and many of the big ranches down there were buying, often planning to sell the rustled cattle they bought back across the border.

It was almost midafternoon before the two riders rounded the shoulder of rock and reined in, looking down the main street of the rickety little town of Apple Cañon. Kilkenny halted his horse and studied the situation. There were four clapboard buildings on one side of the street, three on the other.

"The nearest one is the sawbones," Rusty explained. "He's a renegade from somewheres, but a good doc. Next is the livery stable and blacksmith shop all in one. The long building next door is the bunkhouse. Forty men can sleep there, and usually do. The place after that is Bert Polti's. He lives there with Joe Deagan and Tom Murrow. On the right side the nearest building is Bill Sadler's place. Bill is a gambler. Did a couple of stretches for forgery, too, they say. He cooks up any kind of documents you want. After his place is the big joint of Apple Cañon, the Border Bar. That's Nita's place. She runs it herself. The last house, the one with the flowers around, is Nita's. They say no man ever entered the place. You see"—Rusty glanced at Lance—"Nita's straight, though there's been some has doubted it from time to time. But Nita, she puts 'em right."

"And the place up on the cliffs beyond the town?" Kilkenny wondered. "Who lives there?"

"Huh?" Rusty scowled his puzzlement. "Where you mean?"

Kilkenny pointed. High on a rocky cliff, in a place that seemed to be secure from all but the circling eagles, he could dimly perceive the outline of some sort of a structure. Even in the bright light, with the sun falling fully on the cliff, it was but a vague suggestion. Yet, even as he looked, he caught a flash of light reflecting from something.

"Whoever lives there is a careful man," Kilkenny said dryly. "He's lookin' us over with a glass!"

Rusty was disgusted. "Well, I'll be hanged! I been here three times before, and once stayed five days, and never knowed that place was there."

Kilkenny nodded understandingly. "I'll bet a pretty you can't see it from the town. I just wonder who it is who's so careful? Who wants to know who comes to Apple Cañon? Who can hide up there and remain unknown?"

"You think . . . ?"

"I don't think anything . . . yet. But I mean to find out, some way. I'm a curious *hombre*, Gates."

CHAPTER SEVEN

Kilkenny was in the lead by a dozen paces as the two rode slowly down the street. A man sitting before the Border Bar turned his head and said something through the window, but aside from that there was no movement.

Yet Kilkenny saw a man with a rifle in some rocks at the end of the street, and there was a man with a rifle in the blacksmith shop. The town, he thought grimly, was well guarded.

They walked their horses to the hitching rail and dismounted. The man sitting on the porch looked at them curiously and spat off the end of the porch. His eyes dropped to Kilkenny's tied-down guns, then strayed to his face. His attention seemed to sharpen, and for an instant his eyes wavered to Rusty.

They stepped up on the porch and Kilkenny pushed through the batwing doors. Rusty loitered on the porch, brushing dust from his clothes.

"Travelin's dry business," he muttered.

"Risky, too," the watcher replied softly. "You're askin' for trouble comin' here with him. The word's out."

"For me, too, then," Rusty said. "We're ridin' together."

"Like that, huh? Can't help you none, cowboy."

"Ain't askin'. Just keep out of the way."

Rusty stepped inside. Kilkenny was standing at the bar. The bartender was leaning on the bar farther down, doing nothing. He was pointedly ignoring them.

As Rusty stepped through the doors, he heard Kilkenny say

in a deceptively mild voice: "I'd like a drink."

The bartender did not move a muscle, and gave no evidence that he heard.

"I'd like a drink," Kilkenny said, and his voice was louder.

The three men sitting in the room were covertly watching. Two of them sat against the west and south walls. The third man was across the room, almost behind Kilkenny, and against the east wall. The bar itself covered most of the north wall except where a door opened at one end. It apparently led to a back room.

"I'm askin' once more," Kilkenny said. "I'd like a drink."

The burly bartender turned toward him then, and his stare was hard, ugly.

"I don't hear you, stranger," he said insultingly. "I don't hear you, and I don't know you."

What happened then was to make legend in the border country. Kilkenny turned and his hand shot out. It grasped the bartender's shirt collar, and jerked—so hard that the bartender slid over the bar and crashed on the floor outside of it.

He hit the floor all sprawled out, then came up with a choking cry of anger. But Kilkenny was ready for him. A sharp left lanced at the bartender's eye, and a wicked right hook in the ribs made his mouth drop open. Then Kilkenny stepped in with a series of smashing, bone-crushing punches that pulped the big man's face and made him stagger back, desperately trying to protect his face with crossed arms. But Kilkenny was remorseless. He whipped a right to the midsection to bring the bigger man's arms down, then hooked a left to the chin that dropped the bartender to all fours.

Stopping quickly, Kilkenny picked the man up and smashed a looping right to the chin. The bartender staggered back across the room and hit the floor in a heap against the far wall.

It was over so suddenly, and Big Ed Gardner, the barkeep,

was whipped so quickly and thoroughly that it left the astonished gunmen present staring. Before they could get set for it, Kilkenny sprang back.

"All right!" Kilkenny's voice cracked like a whip in the dead silence of the room. "If you want Kilkenny, turn loose your dogs!"

The name rang like a challenge in the room, and the three men started. The gunman against the west wall touched his lips with a nervous tongue. In his own mind he was sure of one thing. If they went through with their plan he himself was going to die. No one had told them the man they were facing was Kilkenny.

It caught them flat-footed. They sat deathly still, their faces stiff. Then, slowly, the man against the south wall began letting his hand creep away from his guns.

"All right, then," Kilkenny said evenly. "What was you to do here? Gun me down?"

Nobody spoke, and suddenly Kilkenny's gun was in his hand. How it got there no man could say. There was no flicker in his eyes, no dropping of his shoulder, but suddenly his hand was full, and they were looking down the barrel of the .45.

"Talk," Kilkenny said. "You, against the west wall. Tell me who sent you here, and what you was to do. Tell me, or I start shootin' your ears!"

The man swallowed, then wet his lips. "We wasn't to kill you," he said hoarsely. "We was to make you a prisoner."

Kilkenny smiled then. "All right. Mexico's south of here. Travel!"

The three men hit the door in a lump, struggled madly, then all three got out, swung onto their horses, and hit the road on a run.

A rifle cracked outside. Kilkenny stiffened, and stared at Rusty. It rang out twice more. Two neat, evenly spaced shots!

Kilkenny stepped quickly to a place beside the window. One of the fleeing gunmen had been shot down near the end of the street. The others, at almost equal distances, lay beyond.

"Who done that?" Rusty questioned.

"Evidently the boss don't like failure," Kilkenny suggested, thin-lipped. He shrugged. "Well, I still want a drink. Guess I'll have to pour it myself."

"It won't be necessary," said a smooth feminine voice.

Both men turned, startled.

A girl stood at the end of the bar, facing them. She stood erect, her chin lifted a little, one hand resting on the bar. Her skin was the color of old ivory, her hair jet black and gathered in a loose knot at the nape of her neck. But it was her eyes that were most noticeable—and her mouth. Her eyes were hazel, with tiny flecks of a darker color, and they were large, and her lashes were long. Her lips were full, but beautiful, and there was a certain wistfulness in her face, a strange elusive charm that prevented the lips from being sensual. Her figure would have wrung a gasp from a marble statue, for it was seductively curved, and, when she moved, it was with a sinuous grace that had no trace of affectation.

She came forward, and Kilkenny found himself looking into the most amazingly beautiful eyes he had ever seen.

"I am Nita Riordan," she said. "Could I pour you a drink?"

Kilkenny's expression did not change. "Nita Riordan," he said quietly, "you could."

She poured two drinks and handed one to each of them. She did not glance at Big Ed who was beginning to stir on the floor.

"It seems you have had trouble," she said.

"A little . . . hardly worth mentionin'," Kilkenny said with a shrug. "Not so much trouble as any man would cheerfully go through to meet a girl like you."

"You are gallant, *señor*," Nita said, looking directly into his eyes. "Gallantry is always pleasant, and especially so here, where one finds it so seldom."

"Yes," Kilkenny said quietly, "and I am only gallant when I am sincere."

She looked at him quickly, as though anxious to find something in his face. Then she looked away quickly. "Sincerity is difficult to find in the Live Oak, *señor*," she said. "It has little value here."

"It still has value to some," he said, letting his eyes meet hers. "It has to me." He looked down at Big Ed. "I don't like to fight," he said slowly, "but sometimes it is necessary."

Her eyes flashed. "That is not sincere, *señor!*" she retorted severely. "No man who did not like to fight could have done *that!*" With a gesture she indicated Big Ed's face. "Perhaps it is that you like to fight, but do not like *having* to fight. There is a difference."

"Yes." He hitched his guns a little, swallowed his whiskey at a gulp, and looked back at her. "Nita Riordan," he asked quietly, "who is the man in the cliff house above Apple Cañon?"

Her eyes widened a little, then her face set in hard lines. He saw her lips part a little, and saw her quick breath.

"I cannot answer that, *señor*," she said. "If there is a man there, he would resent it. You saw what happened to three who failed? I would not like to die, *señor*. There is much joy in living, even here where there are only outlaws and thieves. Even here the world can be bright, *señor*. For a cause, I can die. For nothing, no. To tell you now would be for nothing."

"They told me you were the boss at Apple Cañon," Kilkenny suggested.

"Perhaps. Things are not always what they seem, *señor.*"

"Then I'll go talk to the man on the cliff," Kilkenny said. "I'll ask him what he wants with Kilkenny, and why he prefers me alive rather than dead."

"Kilkenny?" Nita's eyes widened, and she stepped closer, her eyes searching his face. "You?"

"Yes. Are you surprised?"

She looked up at him, her eyes wide and searching. "I heard long ago, Kilkenny, that you were a good man. I heard that your guns spoke only when the need was great."

"I've tried to keep it that way."

"And you ride alone, Kilkenny?"

"I do.

"And are you never lonely, *señor?* For me, I have found it sometimes lonely."

He looked at her, and suddenly something in his eyes seemed to touch her with fire. He saw her eyes widen a little, and her lips part as though in wonderment. Kilkenny took a half step forward, and she seemed to lean to meet him. Then he stopped abruptly, and turned quickly, almost roughly away.

"Yes," he said somberly, "it has been lonely. It will be more so, now."

He turned abruptly toward the door and had taken three strides when her voice caught him.

"No! Not now to the cliff, *señor.* The time is not now. There will be many guns. Trust me, *señor,* for there will be another time." She stepped closer to him. "That one will be enough for you, *señor,* without others. He is a tiger, a fiend. Perdition knows no viciousness such as his, and he hates you. Why, I do not know, but he hates you with a vindictive hatred, and he will not rest until he kills you. Go now, and quickly. He will not shoot you if you ride away. He wants to face you, *señor.* Why, I do not know."

Kilkenny stopped and turned toward her, his green eyes soft, and strangely warm.

"Nita," he said softly, "I will ride away. He may be the man you love. Mebbe you're protectin' him, yet I don't believe either had dreamed. It was becoming one of the biggest things he had ever walked into. One thing, at least—he had proved to himself that Steele and Lord were out of it. Now if he could bring them to peace with Mort Davis, the only thing left would be to fight it out with the mysterious boss of the gang.

Somehow, more and more, he was beginning to feel that there was more behind this plan than he imagined. This didn't seem like even a simple rustling scheme. Try as he might, he couldn't fit any man into it who he knew. Nor any he had heard of. Yet the fact remained that the leader knew him. Gun experts were as much a part of the West as Indians or cows. It was not an accident that there were so many. And they were, good and bad, essential to the making of the West. Kilkenny was one of the few who saw his own place in the scheme of things clearly. He knew just exactly what he meant, what he was.

Billy the Kid, Pat Garrett, Wes Hardin, Hickok, Ben Thompson, Tom Smith, Earp, Masterson, Tilghman, John Selman, and all the rest were a phase. Most of them cleared out badmen, opened up the West. They fought Indians and they were the tough, outer bark of the pioneering movement. The West was a raw country, and raw men came to it, but there had to be peace. These men, lawless as many of them were, were also an evidence of the coming of law and order, for many of them became sheriffs or marshals, became men who made the West safer to live in.

There could be an end to strife. It was not necessary to go on killing. It could be controlled, and one way to control it was to put the law in the hands of a strong man. Often he was himself a badman, and sometimes he killed the wrong man. But by and large, he kept many other gunmen from killing many more men, and brought some measure of order to the West. Yet this new outlaw leader, this mysterious man upon the cliff, this man who seemed to be pulling the strings from behind the scenes was not

of them things. I'll trust you, Nita. It might be said that a man who trusts a woman is one who writes his name upon water, but I'll take the chance."

He stepped quickly from the door and walked to the buckskin. Gates, only a step behind, also swung into saddle. They rode out of town at a rapid trot.

"Whew!" Rusty Gates stared at Kilkenny. "Mister, when you try, you shore get results. I never saw Nita Riordan like she was today. Every man along the border's had ideas about her. She's hosswhipped a couple, knifed one, and Brigo killed a couple. But today I'd 'a' swore she was goin' t' walk right into your arms."

Kilkenny shrugged. "Never put too much weight on a woman's emotions, Rusty. They ain't reliable. . . ."

Behind them, in the saloon at Apple Cañon, a door slowly opened. The man who stood in the door looking at Big Ed was even larger than the bartender. He seemed to fill the open door, seemed huge, almost too big to be human. Yet there was nothing malformed about him. He was big, but powerfully, splendidly built, and his Indian face was dark and strangely handsome. He moved down the bar with no more noise than a sliding of wind along the floor, and stopped close to Big Ed.

The bartender turned his battered, bloody face toward him.

"No," Brigo said softly, "you will not betray the *señorita*." His black eyes were dark with intent as he stared into Big Ed's. "If one word of this reaches *him*, I kill you! And when I kill you, *amigo mío*, it will not be nice, the way I kill."

"I ain't talkin'," Big Ed said gruffly through battered lips. "I had enough."

CHAPTER EIGHT

Nita was standing in her garden, one hand idly fingering a rose, when Brigo came through the hedge. He looked at her, and his lips parted over perfect teeth.

"You have found him, *señorita*," he murmured. "I see that. You have found this man for whom you waited."

She turned quickly. "Yes, Jaime. It is he. But has he found me?"

"Did you not see his face? His eyes? *Sí, señorita,* Jaime think he find you, too. He is a strong man, that one. Perhaps"—he canted his head speculatively—"so strong as Jaime."

"But what of *him?*" Nita protested. "He will kill him. He hates him."

"*Sí,* he hates. But he will not kill. I think now something new has come. This man, this Kilkenny. He is not the same." Brigo nodded thoughtfully. "I think soon, *señorita,* I return to my home. . . ."

Trailing a few yards behind Kilkenny, Rusty Gates stared up at the wall of the valley. A ragged, pine-spread slope fell away to a rocky cliff, and the sandy wash that ran at the base of it. It was a wild, lonely country. Thinking back over what he knew of this country, he began to see that what Kilkenny had said was the truth. Someone had planned to engineer the biggest rustling plot in Western history.

With this Live Oak country under one brand, cattle could be eased across its range and poured down through the mouth of the funnel into Mexico. By weeding the bigger herds carefully, they might bleed them for years without anyone finding out what was happening. On ranges where cattle were numbered in thousands, a few head from each ranch would not be missed, but in the aggregate it would be an enormous number. This was not the plan of a moment. It was no cowpuncher needing a few extra dollars for a blow-out. This was a steal on the grand scale. It was the design of a man with a brain, and with ruthless courage. Remembering the three men dead back at Apple Cañon, Rusty could see even more. The boss, whoever he was, would kill without hesitation, and on any scale.

Kilkenny was doing some thinking, too. The leader, whoever he was, was a man who knew him. Slowly and carefully he began to sift his past, trying to recall who it might be. Dale Shafter? No, Shafter was dead. He had been killed in the Sutton-Taylor feud. Anyway, he wasn't big enough for this. Card Benton? Too small. A small-time rustler and gambler. One by one he sifted their names, and man after man cropped up in his mind, men who had never rustled, men who were gamblers and gunslingers, men who had cold nerve and who were killers. But somehow none of them seemed to be the type he wanted. And who had fired at him that night in the hollow as he waited for Mort Davis? Who had killed Sam Carter? Was it the same man? Was he the leader? Kilkenny doubted it. This man wanted him alive, and that one had tried to kill him. Indeed, the man had left him for dead. Someone, too, had killed Joe Wilkins. That would take some looking into.

Kilkenny walked his horse down a weathered slide, and crossed a wash. The trail led through a low place walled on each side by low, sandy hills, covered with mesquite, bunch grass, and occasional prickly pear. This job of saving Davis's place for him was turning into something bigger than Lance Kilkenny

one of these. He was different, strange.

Shadows grew longer as the sun sank behind the painted hills, and a light breeze came from the south, blowing up from Mexico. There was a faint smell of dust in the air. Kilkenny glanced at Gates.

"Somebody fogged it along this trail not so long ago," he said. "Somebody who wanted to get some place in a hurry."

"Yeah." Rusty nodded. "And that don't mean anything good for us."

"Whoever the big mogul in this game is," Kilkenny said thoughtfully, "he will try to increase the trouble between Steele and Lord without delay."

"The worst of it is we don't know what he'll do, or where he'll strike next," Gates said.

They were riding at a steady trot toward Botalla when they saw a rider winging it toward them. Rusty flagged him down.

"Hey, what's the rush?" he demanded.

"All tarnation's busted loose!" the rider shouted excitedly. "Lord's hay was set afire, and Steele's fence cut. Some of Lord's boys had a runnin' fight with two of Steele's men, and in town there have been two gunfights!"

"Anybody killed?" Kilkenny demanded anxiously.

"Not yet. Two men wounded on Steele's side!" The cowboy put spurs to his horse and raced off into the night toward the Steele Ranch.

"Well, there goes your cattle war!" Rusty said. "This'll make Lincoln County look like nothin' at all! What do we do now?"

"Stop it, that's what."

Kilkenny whipped the buckskin around and in a minute they were racing down the road toward Botalla.

The main street was empty and as still as death, when they dashed up, but there were lights in the Spur, and more lights in the bigger Trail House. Kilkenny swung down, loosened his guns in their holsters, and walked through the batwing doors of the Trail House.

Men turned quickly at his approach, and their voices died down. He glanced from one to the other, and his eyes narrowed.

"Any Steele men here?" he demanded. Two men stepped forward, staring at him, hesitant, but ready for anything.

"We're from Steele's," one said. "What about it?"

"There'll be no war," Kilkenny said flatly. "Neither of you men is firin' a shot at a Lord man tonight. You hear?"

The cowpuncher who had spoken, a hard-bitten man with a scarred face, grinned, showing broken yellow teeth. "You mean, if I get shot at, I don't fight back? Don't be foolish, *hombre!* If I feel like fightin', I'll fight. Nobody tells me what to do."

Kilkenny's eyes narrowed. "I'm tellin' you." His voice cracked like a whip. "If you shoot, better get me first. If not, I'm comin' after you."

The man's face paled. "Then you talk to them Lord men," he persisted stubbornly, backing off a little. "I ain't anxious for no gunslingin'!"

Kilkenny wheeled and crossed to the Spur. Shoving the doors open, he stepped in and issued the same ultimatum to the Lord men. Several of them appeared relieved. But one man got up and walked slowly down the room toward Kilkenny.

Lance saw it coming. He stood still, watching the man come closer and closer. He knew the type. This man was fairly good with a gun but he wanted a reputation like Kilkenny's, and figured this was the time to get it. Yet there was a lack of certainty in the man's mind. He was coming, but he wasn't sure. Kilkenny was. No man had ever outshot him. He had the confidence given him by many victories.

"I reckon, Kilkenny," the Lord cowpuncher said, "it's time somebody called you. I'm shootin' who I want to, and I ain't takin' orders from you. I hear you're fast. Well, fill your hand!"

He dropped into a gunman's crouch, then froze and his mouth dropped open. He gulped, then swallowed. The gun in Kilkenny's hand was leveled at the pit of his stomach.

Somehow, in the gunfights he'd had before, it had never happened like that. There had been a moment of tenseness, then both had gone for their guns. But this had happened so suddenly. He had expected nothing like that heavy .45 aimed at his stomach, with the tall, green-eyed man standing behind it.

It came to him abruptly that all he had to do to die was drop his hand. All at once, he didn't want to die. He decided that being a gun slick wasn't any part of his business. After all, he was a cowpuncher.

Slowly, step by step, he backed up. Then he swallowed again. "Mister," he said, "I reckon I ain't the *hombre* I thought I was. I don't think there'll be any trouble with the Steele boys tonight."

Kilkenny nodded. "No need for trouble," he said quietly. "There's too much on this range, anyway."

He spun on his heel and walked from the barroom.

For an instant all was still, then the big cowpuncher looked around, and shook his head in amazement.

"Did you see him drag that iron?" he asked pleadingly. "Where the devil did he get it from? I looked, and there it was!"

There was silence for a long time, then one man said sincerely: "I heerd he was gun swift, but nothin' like that. Men, that's Kilkenny!"

Rusty Gates grabbed Kilkenny as he left the Spur.

"Kilkenny," he said, "there's a stranger rode in today. He asked for you. Got somethin' to tell you, he says. Hails from El Paso!"

"El Paso?" Kilkenny scowled. "Who could want to see me from there?"

Gates shrugged. "Purty well lickered, I hear." He lit a smoke.

"But he ain't talkin' fight. Just insists on seein' you."

"Where is he now?"

Kilkenny was thoughtful. El Paso. He hadn't been in El Paso since the Weber fight. Who could want to see him from there?

"He was at the Trail House," Gates said. "Come in just after you took off. Tall, rangy feller. Looks like a cowhand, all right. I mean, he don't look like a gunslinger."

They stepped down off the walk, and started across the street. They had taken but three steps when they heard the sharp rap of a shot. Clear, and ringing in the dark street. A shot, and then another.

"The Trail House!" Gates yelled, and broke into a run.

Kilkenny made the door two steps ahead of him, shoved it open, and stepped in. A cowpuncher lay on his face on the floor, a red stain growing on the back of his shirt. A drawn gun lay near his hand. He was dead.

Slowly Kilkenny looked up. Bert Polti stood across the man's body, a smoking gun in his fist. He looked at Kilkenny and his eyes narrowed. Kilkenny could see the calculation in his eyes, could see the careful estimate of the situation. He had a gun out, and Kilkenny had not drawn. But there was Gates, and in his own mind, reading what the man thought, Kilkenny saw the momentary impulse die.

"Personal fight, Kilkenny," Polti said. "This wasn't no cattle war scrap. He knocked a drink out of my hand. I asked him to apologize. He told me to go to thunder and I beat him to it."

Kilkenny's eyes went past Polti to a cowpuncher from the Lord ranch.

"That right?" he demanded.

"Yeah," the cowpuncher said slowly, his expression unchanging, "that's about what happened."

Polti hesitated, then holstered his weapon and walked outside.

CHAPTER NINE

Several men started to remove the body, and Kilkenny walked to the bar. Looking at the liquor in his glass, he heard Rusty speaking to him softly.

"The *hombre* that got hisself killed," Rusty said, "he was the one lookin' for you."

Kilkenny's eyes caught the eyes of the cowpuncher who had corroborated Polti and, with an almost imperceptible movement of the head, brought the man to the bar.

"You tell me," Kilkenny said. "What happened?"

The cowpuncher hesitated. "Ain't healthy to talk around here," he said doubtfully. "See what happened to one *hombre?* Well, he's only one."

"You don't look like you'd scare easy," Kilkenny said dryly. "You afraid of Polti?"

"No." The cowpuncher faced Kilkenny. "I ain't afraid of him, or of you, either, for that matter. Just ain't healthy to talk. Howsoever, while what Polti said was the truth, it looked powerful like to me that Polti deliberately bumped the cowboy's elbow, that he deliberately drew him into a fight."

"What was the 'puncher sayin'? Anythin' to rile Polti?"

"Not that I know of. He just said he had him a story to tell that would bust this country wide open. He did him a lot of talkin', I'd say."

So! Bert Polti had picked a quarrel with the man who had a message for Kilkenny, a man who said he could bust this country wide open. Kilkenny thought rapidly. What had the man known? And why from El Paso? Suddenly a thought occurred to him.

Finishing his drink, he said out of the corner of his mouth: "Stick around and keep your eyes open, Rusty. If you can, pick up Polti and stay close to him."

Stepping from the Trail House, Kilkenny walked slowly down the street, keeping to the shadows. Then he crossed the alley to the hardware store, and walked down its wall, then along the corral, and around it. He moved carefully, keeping out of sight until he reached the hotel.

There was no one in sight on the porch, and the street was empty. Kilkenny stepped up on the porch and through the door. His action seemed leisurely, to attract no attention, but he wasted no time. The old man who served as clerk was dozing behind the desk, and the proprietor, old Sam Duval, was stretched out on a leather settee in the wide, empty lobby. Kilkenny turned the worn account book that served as register, and glanced down the list of names. It was a gamble, and only a gamble.

It was the fifth name down:

Jack B. Tyson, El Paso, Texas.

The room was number 22. Kilkenny went up the stairs swiftly and silently. There was no sound in the hall above. Those who wanted to sleep were already snoring, and those who wanted the bright lights and red liquor were already at the Trail House or the Spur.

Somewhere in his own past, Kilkenny now felt sure, lay the secret of the man in the cliff house, and this strange rider out of the past who had been killed a short time before might be a clue. Perhaps—it was only a slim chance—there was something in his war bag that would be a clue, something to tell the secret of his killing. For of one thing Kilkenny was certain—the killing of Tyson had been deliberate, and not the result of a barroom argument.

The hallway was dark, and he felt his way with his feet, then when safely away from the stair head, he struck a match. The room opposite him was number 14. In a few minutes he tried again, and this time he found room 22.

Carefully he dropped a hand to the knob and turned it softly. Like a ghost he entered the room, but even as he stepped in, he saw a dark figure rise from bending over something at the foot of the bed. There was a quick stab of flame, and something burned along his side. Then the figure wheeled and plunged through the open window to the shed roof outside. Kilkenny went to the window and snapped a quick shot at the man as he dropped from the roof edge. But even as he fired, he knew he had missed.

For an instant he thought of giving chase, then the idea was gone. The man, whoever he was, would be in the crowds around the Spur or the Trail House within a matter of minutes, and it would be a fool's errand. In the meantime, he would lose what he sought here.

There was a pounding on the steps, and he turned, lighting the lamp. The door was slammed open, and the clerk stood there, his old chest heaving. Behind him, clutching a shotgun, was Duval.

"Here!" Duval bellowed. "What the consarn you doin' in there? And who's a-shootin'? I tell you I won't have it!"

"Take it easy, dad," Kilkenny said, grinning. "I came up to have a look at Tyson's gear and caught somebody goin' through it. He shot at me."

"What right you got to go through his gear your ownself?" Duval snapped suspiciously.

"He was killed in the Trail House. Somebody told me he had

a message for me. I was lookin' for it."

"Well, I reckon he ain't fit to do no kickin'," Duval admitted grudgingly, "and I heard him say he had a word for Kilkenny. All right, go ahead, but don't be shootin'! Can't sleep noways."

He turned and stumped down the narrow stairs behind the clerk.

A thorough examination of the drifting cowpuncher's gear got Kilkenny exactly nowhere. It was typical of a wandering cowpuncher of the period. There was nothing more, and nothing less.

There was still no solution, and out on the plains he knew there had been no settlement of the range war situation. His own warnings had averted a clash tonight, but he could not be everywhere, and sooner or later trouble would break open on the range. Already, in other sections, there was fighting over the introduction of wire. Here, the problem was made worse by the plot of the rustlers, or what he believed was their plot.

He could see a few things. For one, the plan had been engineered by a keen, intelligent, ruthless man. That he had already decided. It would have gone off easily had he not suddenly, because of Mort Davis, been injected into the picture. The fact that the mysterious man behind the scenes hated him was entirely beside the point, even though that hate had evidently become a major motive in the mysterious man's plans.

Well, what did he have? Somewhere behind the scenes were the Brockmans. Neither of them was a schemer. Both were highly skilled killers, clansmen of the old school, neither better nor worse than any other Western gunmen except that they fought together. It was accepted by everyone that they would always fight together. The Brockmans he did not know. From the beginning he had accepted the fact that someday he would kill them. That he did not doubt. Few of the real gunfighters doubted. To doubt would have been to fail. There was the famous case of the duel between Dave Tutt and Bill Hickok as an example. Hickok shot Tutt and turned to get the drop on Tutt's friends before the man shot had even hit the ground. Bill had known he was dead.

The Brockmans no doubt felt as secure in the belief they would win as Kilkenny did. Somebody had to be wrong, but he could not make himself believe that was important. It was something he would have to live through, and it in no way could affect the solution of the plot on which he was working. True, he might be killed, but if so the solution wouldn't matter, anyway.

Every way he looked at it, the only actual member of the outlaw crew he could put a finger on was Bert Polti, and there was a measure of doubt there. He had not seen Polti at Apple Cañon. The man had a house there, but apparently spent most of his time at Botalla. Polti might have killed Wilkins and Carter. It seemed probable he had. Yet there was no proof. No positive proof.

Again and again Kilkenny returned to the realization that he must go up to the cliff house at Apple Cañon. He was not foolish enough to believe he could do it without danger. He had none of the confidence there that he would have in facing any man with a gun, for in the attack on the cliff house, an attack must be made alone. There were too many intangibles, too many imponderables, too many things one could not foresee. Lord and Steele might postpone their fighting for a day or two. They might never fight, but the problem of Lost Creek Valley would not be settled, and the man at Apple Cañon would try to force the issue at the first moment.

Standing in the dimly lit room, Kilkenny let his gaze drift about him. He had turned then, to go, when an idea hit him. The man who had fired at him before, and who had killed Carter, had stopped on the spot to reload. A careful man. But then, a smart man with a gun always was.

Carefully Kilkenny began to search the room, knowing even as he did that the search would be useless, for the man had left too quickly to have left anything. Then he went down the stairs and out back. With painstaking care, and risking a shot from the dark, he examined the ground. He found footsteps, and followed them.

Sixty feet beyond the hotel, he found what he sought. The running man had dropped the shell here, and shoved another into the chamber. Kilkenny picked up the brass shell. A glance told him what he had half expected to find. The unseen gunman was the man who had killed Sam Carter.

"Found somethin'?"

He straightened swiftly. It was Gates, standing there, his hand on his pistol butt, staring at him.

"A shell. Where's Polti?"

"Left town for Apple Cañon, ridin' easy, takin' his time."

"You been with him like I said?" Kilkenny demanded.

"Yeah." Rusty nodded. "He didn't do that shootin' a while ago, if that's what you mean. I heard the shootin', then somebody come in and told us you was playin' target down here, and I'd had Polti within ten feet of me ever since you left me."

Kilkenny rubbed his jaw and stared gloomily into the darkness. So it wasn't Bert Polti. The theory that had been half formed in his mind that Polti was himself the unseen killer, and a close agent of the man on the cliff, was shattered.

Suddenly a new thought came to him. What of Rusty? Where had Rusty Gates been? Why had Rusty joined him? Was it from sheer love of battle and admiration for him, Kilkenny? Or for some deeper purpose?

He shook his head. He would be suspecting himself if this continued. Turning, followed by Gates, he walked slowly back to the street. He felt baffled, futile. Wherever he turned, he was stopped. There were shootings and killings, then the killer vanished.

The night was wearing on, and Kilkenny mounted the buckskin and rode out into the desert. He had chosen a place, away from the town, for his camp. Now he rode to it and unsaddled Buck. Within a few minutes he had made his camp. He lit no fire, but the moon was coming up.

It was just clearing the tops of the ridges when he heard a ghost-like movement. Instantly he rolled over behind a boulder and slid his six-gun into his hand. On the edge of the wash, not fifteen feet away, a man was standing.

"Don't shoot, Kilkenny," a low voice drawled easily. "This is a friendly call."

"All right," Kilkenny said, rising to his full height. "Come on up, but watch it. I can see in the dark just as well as the light."

The man walked forward and stopped within four feet of Kilkenny. He was smiling a little.

"Sorry to run in on you thisaway," he said pleasantly, "but I wanted a word or two in private, and you're a right busy man these days."

Kilkenny waited. There was something vaguely familiar about the man. Somewhere, sometime he had seen him.

"Kilkenny," the man said, "I've heard a lot about you. Heard you're a square shooter, and a good man to tie to. Well, I like men like that. I'm Lee Hall."

Lee Hall! The famous Texas Ranger, the man known as Red Hall who had brought law and order to more than one wild Texas cow town, and who was known throughout the border regions! He walked around a little, then stopped.

"Kilkenny," he said slowly, "I suppose you're wonderin' why I'm here? Well, as I said, I've heard a lot about you. I need some help, and I reckon you're the man. What's been happenin' down here?"

Briefly Kilkenny sketched in the happenings since his arrival, and what had happened before, from what he had heard. He advanced his theories about Apple Cañon.

"Nita Riordan?" Hall nodded. "I knew her old man. He came out from the East. Good man. Hadn't lived in Carolina long, came there from Virginia, but good family, and a good man. Heard he had a daughter."

"What did you want me to do?" Kilkenny asked.

"Go ahead with what you're doin', and keep this cattle war down. I'm puttin' up wire on my own place now, and we're havin' troubles of our own. If you need any help, holler. But you're bein' deputized here and now. Funny thing," Hall suggested thoughtfully, "you tellin' me about the killin' of Wilkins and Carter. These ain't the first of the kind from the Live Oak country. For the past six years now people have been gettin' mysteriously shot down here. In fact, Chet Lord's half-brother was drygulched, and not far from Apple Cañon. Name of Destry King. Never found who did it, and there didn't seem any clue. But he told me a few days before he died that he thought he knew who the killer in the neighborhood was."

CHAPTER TEN

Hall left after over two hours of talk. Kilkenny stretched out with his saddle for a pillow, and stared up at the stars.

Could it be there was some other plot, something that had been begun before the present one? Could the old killings be connected with the new? There was only a hint. Destry King, half-brother to Chet Lord, had been killed when he had thought he had a clue. Had he confided in his half-brother?

It was high time, Kilkenny thought, that he had a talk with Chet Lord. So far circumstances had conspired to keep him so occupied that there had been no chance, and his few messages had been sent through Steve.

Long before daylight Kilkenny rolled out of his blankets and saddled up. He headed out for Cottonwood and the railroad and arrived at the small station to find no one about but the stationmaster. Carefully he wrote out three messages. One of them was to El Paso, and one to Dodge. The third was to a friend in San Antonio, a man who had lived long in the Live Oak country, and who before that had lived in Missouri.

When he left Cottonwood, he cut across country to the Apple Cañon trail and headed for the Chet Lord Ranch. He was riding through a narrow defile among the rocks, when suddenly he saw two people riding ahead. They were Tana Steele and Victor Bonham.

"Howdy," he said, touching his Stetson. "Nice day."

Tana reined in and faced him.

"Hello," she said evenly. "Are you still as insulting as ever?"

"Do you mean, am I still as stubborn about spoiled girls as ever?" He grinned. "Bonham, this girl's shore enough a wildcat. Plenty of teeth, too, although pretty."

Bonham laughed, but Kilkenny saw his eyes drop to the tied-down guns. When they lifted, there was a strange expression in them. Then Bonham reined his horse around a bit, broadside to Kilkenny.

"Going far?" Bonham asked quietly.

"Not far."

"Chet Lord's, I suppose? I hear he's not a pleasant man to do business with."

Kilkenny shrugged. "Doesn't matter much. I do business with 'em, pleasant or otherwise."

"Aren't you the man who killed the Weber brothers?" Bonham asked. "I heard you did. I should think it would bother you."

"Bother me?" Kilkenny shrugged. "I never think of it much. The men I kill ask for it, an' they don't worry me much one way or the other."

"It wasn't a matter of conscience," Bonham replied dryly. "I was thinking of Royal Barnes. I hear he was a relative of theirs, and one of the fastest men in the country."

"Barnes?" Kilkenny shrugged. "I never gave him a thought. The Webers asked for it, an' they got it. Why should Barnes ask for anything? I've never even seen the man."

"He might," Bonham said. "And he's fast."

Kilkenny ignored the Easterner and glanced at Tana. She had been sitting there watching him, a curious light in her eyes.

"Ma'am," he said slowly, "did you know Destry King?"

"King?" Tana's eyes brightened. "Oh, certainly. We all knew Des. He was Chet Lord's half-brother. Or rather, step-brother, for they had different parents. He was a grand fellow. I had quite a crush on him when I was fourteen."

"Killed, wasn't he?" Kilkenny asked.

"Yes. Someone shot him from behind some rocks. Oh, it was awful. Particularly as the killer walked up to his body and shot him twice more in the face and twice in the stomach."

Bonham sat listening, and his eyes were puzzled as he looked at Kilkenny. "I don't believe I understand," he said. "I thought you were averting a cattle war, but now you seem curious about an outdated killing."

Kilkenny shrugged. "He was killed from ambush. So were Sam Carter and Joe Wilkins. So were several others. Of course, they all cover quite a period of time, but none of the killin's was ever solved. It looks a bit odd."

Bonham's eyes were keen. He looked as if he had made a discovery. "Ah, I see," he said. "You imply there may be a connection? That the same man may have killed them all? That the present killings weren't part of the range war?"

"I think the present killin's were part of the range war," Kilkenny said positively, "but the way of killin' is like the killin's in them old crimes." He turned to Tana. "Tell me about Des King."

"I don't know why I shouldn't," she said. "As I told you, Des was a wonderful fellow. Everyone liked him. That was what made his killing so strange. He was a fast man with a gun, too, and one of the best riders on the range. Everyone made a lot of Des. Several riders had been shot, then an old miner. I think the first person killed was an old Indian. Old Comanche, harmless enough . . . used to live around the Lord Ranch. Altogether I think there were seven men killed before Des was. He started looking into it, having an idea they were all done by the same man. He told me once that I shouldn't go riding, that I should stay home and not ride in the hills. Said it wasn't safe."

"You rode a good deal as a youngster?"

"Oh, yes. There weren't many children around, and I used to

ride over to talk and play with Steve Lord. Our fathers were good friends then, but it was six miles over rough country to his house then . . . wild country."

"Thanks. I'll be gettin' on. Thanks for the information, ma'am. Glad to have seen you again, Bonham."

Bonham smiled. "I think we may see each other often, Kilkenny."

Suddenly Tana put out her hand. "Really, Kilkenny," she said, "I'm sorry about that first day. I knew you were right that first time, but I was so mad I hated to admit it. I'm sorry."

"Shore." Kilkenny grinned. "But I'm not takin' back what I said about you."

Tana stiffened. "What do you mean?"

"Mean?" He raised his eyebrows innocently. "Didn't I say you were mighty pretty?"

He touched his spurs lightly to the buckskin's flanks and took off at a bound. After a brisk gallop for about a quarter of a mile he slowed down to a walk, busy with his thoughts.

Hall's information had been correct. Des King had had a theory as to who the killer was. He had been steadily tracking him down. Then the killer must have seen how near he was to capture, and had killed King. But what was the thread that connected the crimes? There was no hint of burglary or robbery in any of them. Yet there had to be a connection. The pattern was varied only in the case of King, for he had been shot several times, shot as if the killer had hated him, shot through and through. And why a harmless old Indian? A prospector? Several riders? Kilkenny rode on, puzzling.

Ahead of him the ground dipped into a wide and shallow valley down which led the cattle trail he was following. Nearby were rocks, and a wash not far away.

Kilkenny rolled a smoke and thoughtfully lit it. He flipped the match away and shoved his sombrero back on his head. The situation was getting complicated, and nowhere closer to a solution. The Steele and Lord fight was hanging fire. Twice there had been minor bursts of action, and then both had petered out after his taking a hand, yet it wasn't fooling anybody. The basic trouble was still there, and Davis hadn't been brought together with Steele and Lord.

Above the Live Oak, the country was seething, too. Wire cutters were loose, and fences were torn down nightly. Cattle were being rustled occasionally, but in small bunches. There was no evidence they had come through the Live Oak country and down to Apple Cañon.

Kilkenny had almost reached the Lord ranch house when he saw Steve come riding toward him, a smile on his face. Steve looked closely at Kilkenny, his eyes curious.

"Didn't expect to see you over here," he said. "I figgered you was goin' back to Apple Cañon."

"Apple Cañon?" Kilkenny asked. "Why?"

"Oh, most people who see Nita want to see her again," Steve said. "You lookin' for Dad?"

"That's right. Is he around?"

"Uhn-huh. That's him on the roan hoss."

They rode up to the big man, and Kilkenny was pleased. Chet Lord was typically a cattleman of the old school. Old Chet turned and stared at Kilkenny as he approached, then looked quickly from him to Steve. He smiled and held out his hand.

"Kilkenny, huh? I thought so from the stories I been hearin'."

Lord's face was deeply lined, and there were creases of worry about his eyes. Either the impending cattle war was bothering Chet Lord or something else was. He looked like anything but a healthy man now. Yet it wasn't a physical distress. Something, Kilkenny felt instinctively, was troubling the rancher.

"Been meanin' to see you, Mister Lord," Kilkenny said. "Got to keep you an' Steele off each other's backs. Then get you with

Mort Davis."

"You might get me and Webb together," Lord said positively, "but I ain't hankerin' for no parley with that cow-stealin' Davis."

"Shucks." Kilkenny grinned. "You mean to tell me you never rustled a cow? I'll bet you rustled aplenty in your time. Why, I have myself. I drove a few over the border couple of times when I needed a stake."

"Well, mebbe," said Lord. "But Davis come in and settled on the best piece of cow country around here. Right in the middle of my range."

"Yours or Steele's," Kilkenny said. "What the devil? Did you expect him to take the worst? He's an old buffalo hunter. He hunted through there while you was still back in Missouri."

"Mebbe. But we used this range first."

"How'd you happen to come in here? Didn't like Missouri?"

Chet Lord dropped a hand to the pommel of his saddle and stared at Kilkenny. "That's none of your cussed business, gunman! I come here because I liked it . . . no other reason."

His voice was sharp, irritated, and Kilkenny detected under it that the man was dangerously near the breaking point. But why? What was riding him? What was the trouble?

Kilkenny shrugged. "It don't mean anythin' to me. I don't care why you came here. Or why you stay. By the way, what's your theory about the killin' of Des King?"

Chet Lord's face went deathly pale, and he clutched suddenly, getting a harder grip on the saddle horn. Kilkenny saw his teeth set, and the man turned tortured, frightened eyes at Kilkenny.

"You better get," Lord managed after a minute. "You better get goin' now. If you'll take a tip from a friendly man, keep movin'."

He wheeled his horse and walked it away. For a moment,

Kilkenny watched him, then turned his head to find Steve staring at him, in his eyes that strange, leaping white light Kilkenny had seen once before.

"Don't bother Dad," Steve said. "He ain't been well lately. Not sleepin' good. I think this range war has got him worried."

"Worried?"

"Uhn-huh. We need money. If we lose many cows, we can't pay off some debts we've got."

After a few minutes' talk, Kilkenny turned his buckskin and rode away from the ranch. He rode away in a brown study. Something about Des King had Chet Lord bothered. Was Lord the murderer of his own step-brother? But no! Chet might shoot a man, but he would do it in a fair, stand-up fight. There was no coyote in Chet Lord any more than there was in Webb Steele or Mort Davis.

Chapter Eleven

More and more the tangled skein of the situation became more twisted, and more and more he felt the building up of powerful forces around him, with nothing he could take hold of. He was in serious danger, he knew, yet danger was something he had always known. It was the atmosphere he had breathed since he had gunned his first man in a fair stand-up fight at the age of sixteen.

There was something about Chet Lord's fear that puzzled him. Lord had seemed more to be afraid for him, than for himself. Why? What could have aroused Lord's fear so? And what had made the man so upset? Was he really in debt? Somehow, remembering the place and the fat cattle, and knowing the range as he did, Kilkenny could not convince himself that Steve's statement was true. It was a cover-up for something else. There was fresh paint, all too rare in the Texas of those days, and new barbed wire, and new ranch buildings, and every indication that money was being spent.

Yet somewhere on that range a killer was loose, a strange, fiendish killer. It was unlike the West, a man who struck from ambush, a man who would kill an old Indian, who would ambush a prospector, and who would shoot down lonely riders. Somewhere, in all the welter of background, there was a clue.

Kilkenny lifted his head and stared gloomily down the trail. He was riding back through the shallow valley and down the cattle trail along which he had just traveled. He looked ahead, and for some reason felt uneasy.

Lord's gettin' his fear into me, he told himself grimly. *Still, in a country like this a man's a fool to ride twice over the same trail.*

On the impulse of the moment, he wheeled his horse and took it in two quick jumps for the shelter of the wash. As the horse gathered himself for the second jump, a shot sounded, and Kilkenny felt the whip of the bullet past his head. Then another and another.

But Buck knew what shooting was, and he hit the wash in one more jump and slid into it in a cascade of sand and gravel. Kilkenny touched spurs to the horse and went down the wash on a dead run. That wash took a bend up above. If he could get around that bend in a hurry, he might outflank the killer.

He went around the bend in a rush and hit the ground running, rifle in hand. Flattening himself behind a hummock of sand and sagebrush, he peered through, trying to locate the unseen rifleman. But he moved slightly, trying to see better, and a shot clipped by him, almost burning his face. A second shot kicked sand into his eyes. He slid back into the wash in a hurry.

"The devil!" he exploded. "That *hombre* is wise! Spotted me, did he?"

He swung into saddle and circled farther, then tried again from the bank. Now he could see into the nest of rock where the killer must have waited and from which the first shot had come. There was no one in sight. Then he saw a flicker of movement among the rocks higher up. The killer was stalking him!

Crouching low, he waited, watching a gap in the rocks. Then he saw the shadow of a man, only a blob of darkness from where he huddled, and he fired. It was a quick, snapped shot and it clipped the boulder and ricocheted off into the daylight, whining wickedly.

Then it began—a steady circling. Two riflemen trained in the West, each maneuvering for a good shot, each wanting to kill.

Twice Kilkenny almost got in shots, and then one clipped the rock over his head. An hour passed, and still he had seen nothing. He circled higher among the rocks and, after a long search, found a place where a man had knelt. On the ground nearby was a rifle shell, a shell from a Winchester carbine, Model 1873.

Mebbe that'll help, he told himself. *Ain't too many of 'em around. The Rangers mostly have 'em. And I've got one. I think Rusty still uses his old Sharps, and I expect Webb Steele does. But say!* He stopped, scowling. *Why, Tana Steele has a 'Seventy-Three! Yeah, and if I ain't mistaken, so has Bonham!*

This couldn't continue. Three times now the killer had tried shots at him, if indeed all had been fired by the same man. Bonham was in the vicinity, but why should Bonham shoot at him? Tana Steele was near, also, and Tana might have a streak of revenge in her system. But Chet Lord wasn't far away, either, and there were other men on the range who might shoot. Above all, this was an uncertain country where every man rode with an itch in his trigger finger these days.

One thing was sure. He was no nearer a solution than he had been. He had shells from the killer's six-gun and now from a Winchester 1873. Yet he had no proof beyond a hunch that the attempts at killing had been made by the same man.

The mysterious boss of Apple Cañon apparently had not wanted him killed. Hence, why the attempts now, if he were responsible? Or had the attempts, as he had suspected before, been the work of different men? But if not the Apple Cañon boss, and if not Bert Polti, then who? And why? Who else had cause to kill him?

Yet, so far as he knew, many of the mysterious killings in the past had been done without cause. At least, there had been no reason of which he was aware. Underneath it all, some strange influence was at work, something cruel and evil, something that was not typical of the range country where men settled their disputes face to face.

Kilkenny kept to back trails in making his way back to Botalla. The thing now was to get Steele, Lord, and Davis together and settle their difficulties, if they could be settled. Knowing all three men, and knowing the kind of men they were, he had little doubt of a settlement.

The two bigger cattlemen were range hungry and Davis was stubborn. Like many men, each of them wanted to work his own way, each was a rugged individualist who had yet to learn that many more things are accomplished by co-operation than by solitary efforts.

Botalla lay quietly under the late sun when the buckskin walked down the street. A few men were sitting around, and among them were several cowpunchers from the Lord and Steele spreads. Kilkenny reined in alongside a couple of them. A short cowpuncher with batwing chaps and a battered gray sombrero looked up at him from his seat on the boardwalk, rolled his quid in his jaws, and spat.

"How's it?" he said carefully.

"So-so." Kilkenny shoved his hat back on his head and reached for the makings. "You're Shorty Lewis, ain't you?"

The short cowpuncher looked surprised. "Shore am. How'd you know me?"

"Saw you one time in Austin. Ridin' a white-legged roan horse."

Lewis spat again. "Well, I'll be durned! I ain't had that hoss for three year. You shore got a memory."

Kilkenny grinned and lit his cigarette. "Got to have, livin' like I do. An *hombre* might forget the wrong face!" He drew deeply on the smoke. "Shorty, you ride for Steele, don't you?"

"Been ridin' for him six year," Lewis said. "Before that I was up in the Nations."

"Know Des King?" Kilkenny asked casually.

Lewis got to his feet.

"Just what's on your mind, Kilkenny?" he asked. "Des King was a half-brother of Lord's, but we rode together up in the Nations. He was my friend."

Kilkenny nodded. "I thought mebbe. Lewis, I got me a hunch the *hombre* that killed Wilkins and Carter also killed Des King. I got a hunch that *hombre* tried to kill me."

"But King was killed some time ago," Lewis protested. "Before this fight got started."

"Right. But somebody is ridin' this range that has some other reason for killin' men. Somebody who's cold-blooded and vicious like nobody you ever seen, Shorty. Somebody that's blood-thirstier than an Apache."

"What kind of man would be killin' like that?" Lewis demanded. Then he nodded. "Mebbe you got somethin', feller. Nobody would've shot into Des after he was down, mebbe already dead, except somebody who hated him poison mean, or somebody who loved killin'."

"There was an old Indian killed, and a prospector," reminded Kilkenny. "Know anything about them?"

"Yeah. Old Yellow Hoss was a Comanche. He got to hittin' the bottle purty hard and Chet Lord kept him around and kept him in likker because of some favor the old Injun done for him years ago. Well, one day they found him out on the range, shot in the back. No reason for it, so far's anybody could see. The prospector's stuff had been gone over, but nothin' much was missin' except an old bone-handled knife . . . a Injun scalpin' knife he used to carry. Had no enemies anybody could find. That seems to be the only tie up betwixt 'em."

"Where were they killed?"

"Funny thing, all of 'em were killed betwixt Apple Cañon and Lost Creek Valley. All but one, that is. Des King was killed on the Lord range not far from Lost Creek."

90

Kilkenny nodded. "How about you tellin' Chet to come in tomorrow mornin' for a peace talk, Shorty? I'll get Webb and Mort Davis in."

After he had told some of the Steele hands that he wanted to see Webb, Kilkenny rode down to the general store. Old Joe Frame was selling a bill of goods to Mort Davis's boy. Through him word was sent to Mort.

Rusty was waiting on the boardwalk in front of the Trail House when Kilkenny returned. He looked up and grinned.

"If you swing a loop over all three of 'em," he said, "you're doin' a job, pardner. It'll mean peace in the Live Oak."

"Yes," Kilkenny said dryly, "peace in the Live Oak after the gang at Apple Cañon is rounded up."

Gates nodded. Touching his tongue to a cigarette paper, he looked at Kilkenny. "May not be so hard. You been makin' friends, pardner. Lots of these local men been a-talkin' to me. Frame, Winston, the lawyer, Doc Clyde, Tom Hollins, and some more. They want peace, and they want some law in Botalla. What's more, they'll fight for it. They told me I could speak for 'em, say that when you need a posse, you can dang' soon get it in Botalla."

"Good." Kilkenny nodded with satisfaction. "We'll need it."

"Think any effort'll be made to break up your peace meetin'?" Rusty asked. "I been wonderin' about that."

"I doubt it. Might be. They better not, if they are goin' to try, because I got us a plan."

Morning sunlight bathed the dusty street when the riders from the Steele Ranch came in. There were just Webb, Tana, Weston, and two Steele riders. One of them was Shorty Lewis.

Rusty and Kilkenny were loafing in front of the Trail House.

"She's shore purty," Rusty said thoughtfully, staring after Tana as she rode toward the hotel. "Never saw a girl so purty."

Kilkenny grinned. "Why don't you marry the gal?" he asked. "Old Webb needs him a bright young son-in-law, and Tana's quite a gal. Some spoiled, but I reckon a good strong hand would make quite a woman of her."

"Marry *her?*" Rusty exploded. "She wouldn't look at me. Anyway, I thought mebbe you had your brand on her."

"Not me." Kilkenny shook his head. "Tana's all right, Rusty, but Kilkenny rides alone. No man like me has a right to marry and mebbe break some woman's heart when someday he don't reach fast enough. No, Rusty, I've been ridin' alone, and I'll keep it up. If I was to change, it wouldn't be Tana. I like to tease her a bit, because she's had it too easy with men and with everything, but that's all."

He got up, and together they walked down the street toward the hotel. Webb Steele and Tana were idling about the lobby. In a few minutes, Chet Lord came in, followed by Steve. Then the door opened, and Mort Davis stood there, his tall, lean figure almost blocking the door. He stared bleakly at Steele, then at Lord, and walked across the room to stand before the cold fireplace with his thumbs hooked in his belt.

"Guess we better call this here meetin' to order," Kilkenny suggested, idly riffling a stack of cards. "The way I hear it, Steele an' Lord are disputin' about who fences in Lost Creek, while Mort here is holdin' Lost Creek."

"He's holdin' it," Steele said harshly, "but he ain't got no right to it."

"Easy now," Davis said. "How'd you get that range of your'n, Steele? You just rode in an' took her. Well, that's what I done. Anyway, I figgered on Lost Creek for ten year. I come West with Jack Halloran's wagon train fifteen year ago and saw Lost Creek then."

"Huh?" Webb Steele stiffened. "You rode with Halloran? Why, Tana's mother was Jack Halloran's sister."

Davis stared. "Is that a fact? You all from Jackson County?"

"We shore are! Why, you old coot, why didn't you tell me you was *that* Davis? Jack used to tell us about how you and him. . . ." Webb stopped, looking embarrassed.

"Go right ahead, Steele," Kilkenny said dryly. "I knew if you and Mort ever got together and quit fightin' long enough to have a confab, you'd get along. Same thing with Lord here. Now, listen. There ain't no reason why you three can't get together. You, Steele, are importin' some fine breedin' stock. So is Lord. Mort hasn't got the money for that, but he does have Lost Creek, and he's got a few head of stock. I don't see why you need to do any fencin'. Fence out the upper Texas stock, but keep the Live Oak country, this piece of it, as it is. Somebody has moved into Apple Cañon and has gathered a bunch of rustlers around. Well, they've got to be cleared out. Lock, stock, and barrel. I'm takin' that on myself."

"We need some law here," Webb Steele said suddenly. "How about you becomin' marshal?"

"Not me," Kilkenny said. "I'm a sort of deputy now. Lee Hall dropped by my camp the other night and he gave me this job. Makes it sort of official. But before I leave here, I'm goin' to take care of that bunch at Apple Cañon. Also," he added, "I'm goin' to get the man responsible for all these killin's."

His eyes touched Chet Lord's face as he spoke, and the big rancher's face was ashen.

Steve spoke up suddenly. "You sound as if you believed there's no connection between the killin's and this fight?"

"Mebbe there is, mebbe there isn't. What I think is that the man who's doin' the killin' is the same man who killed Des King, the same who killed old Yellow Horse."

Chapter Twelve

Chet Lord was slumped in his chair and Kilkenny thought he had never seen a man look so old. Tana Steele was looking strange, too, and Kilkenny, looking up suddenly, saw that her face was oddly white and puzzled.

"I think," Kilkenny said, after he had made his disturbing accusation about the mysterious killer, "that Des King knew who the killer was. He was killed to keep him from exposing that rattler, and also, I believe, because the killer hated King."

"Why didn't he tell then?" Steve Lord demanded.

Kilkenny looked at Steve. "Mebbe he did," he said slowly. "Mebbe he did."

"What d' you mean by that?" Webb Steele demanded. "If he told, I never heard nothin' of it."

Kilkenny sat quietly, but he could see the tenseness in Tana's face, the ashen pallor of Chet Lord, slumped in his chair, and Steve's immobile, hard face.

"Des," Kilkenny said slowly, "had a little hang-out in the hills. In a box cañon west of Forgotten Pass. Well, Des kept a diary, an account of his search for the killer. He told Lee Hall that, and Lee told me. Tomorrow I'm goin' to that cabin in the cañon and get that diary. Then I'll know the whole story."

"I think . . . ," Tana began, but got no further because suddenly there was a hoarse yell from the street and the sharp bark of a six-gun. Then a roll of heavy firing.

Kilkenny left his chair with a bound and kicked the door

open. There was another burst of firing as he lunged down the steps. His foot caught and he plunged headlong into the dust, his head striking a rock that lay at the foot of the steps.

Rusty and the others plunged after him. They were just in time to see two big men lunging for their horses while rifles and pistols began to bark from all over town. One of the big men threw up his pistol and blazed away at the group on the porch. Rusty had just time to grab Tana and push her to the porch floor as bullets spattered the hotel wall.

Kilkenny, his head throbbing from the blow of his fall, crawled blindly to his feet, eyes filled with dust. There was a wild rattle of hoof beats, then horses charged by him. One caught him a glancing blow with its shoulder and knocked him flat again. There was another rattle of gunfire, and then it was over.

Kilkenny got to his feet again, wiping the dust from his eyes.

"What was it?" he choked. "What happened?"

Frame had come running up the street from the general store, carrying an old Sharps rifle.

"The Brockmans!" he shouted. "That's who it was! Come to bust up your meetin' and wipe you out, Kilkenny. Jim Weston, Shorty, and the other Steele rider tried to stop 'em."

Webb Steele stepped down, eyes blazing. "So that was the Brockmans that rode by! Cussed near killed my daughter!"

"Yeah," Frame agreed. "They got Weston. Lewis is shot bad, and they got the other boy . . . O'Connor, I think his name was. Weston never had a chance. He dropped his hand for his gun and Cain drilled him plumb center. Abel took Lewis, and they both lowered guns on the last one. It was short and bloody, and I don't think either of them got a scratch."

"This busts it!" Steele shouted. "We'll ride to Apple Cañon and burn that bunch to the ground! They've gone too far!"

Tana Steele was straightening up. She looked at Rusty. "You

saved my life," she said quietly. "If you hadn't thrown yourself in front of me, I might have been killed."

Rusty grinned, and suddenly Kilkenny saw blood on his shirt.

"You better take him inside, Tana," he said. "He's hit."

"Oh!" Tana caught Rusty quickly. "You're hurt!"

"It ain't nothin'," Rusty, said. "Shucks, I. . . ." He slumped limply against the wall.

Steele and Frame picked him up and started inside. The Lords, father and son, headed down the street.

Suddenly Kilkenny heard the porch boards creak, and a low voice, Bert Polti's, spoke.

"All right, Mister Lance Kilkenny, here's where you cash in."

As Kilkenny recognized the voice, he whirled and drew. Polti's gun flamed as Kilkenny turned, and he felt the hot breath of the bullet. Then he fired.

Polti staggered, but caught himself. His head thrust forward, he tried to squeeze off another shot, but the six-gun wouldn't come up. He tried, then tried again, but slowly the gun muzzle lowered, he toppled, and fell headlong.

Steele came charging to the door, gun in hand. He took one look, then holstered his gun.

"Polti, huh? He's had it a comin' for a long time. How come he drew on you?"

Kilkenny explained briefly. Steele nodded. "Figgered with your back turned he had a chance to get you. Well, he didn't make it. Good work, son! You beat the rope for him with that bullet." He looked down at the fallen man. "Plumb center, too. Right through the heart."

Kilkenny looked up. "Steele, get your boys ready and stand by. Have Lord do the same. I'm goin' after the Brockmans myself, and, when I come back, we're goin' to clean up Apple Cañon. Right now the main thing is to get the Brockmans out of the way."

"You goin' after 'em alone?" Steele was incredulous. "They just gunned down three men!"

"Uhn-huh." Kilkenny grinned, without humor. "But there's only two of 'em. I'll go after 'em. You see that somebody takes care of Rusty."

Steele grinned then. "I reckon Tana's doin' that."

A half hour later, stocked with grub for three days, Kilkenny rode out of town on the trail of the Brockmans. For the first half mile they had ridden hard, then had slowed down, saving their horses when they noticed no pursuit. They were both shrewd riders and they would save their horses while confusing their trail.

Three miles from town they had turned from the trail and taken to the rough country toward the lava beds. The trail became steadily more difficult, and wound back and forth across the desert, weaving around clusters of boulders and following dry washes. They had used every trick of desert men to lose their trail, and yet it could be followed. Still, time and again, Kilkenny was compelled to dismount from his horse, search the ground carefully, and follow as much by guess and instinct as by sight or knowledge.

It became evident the Brockmans were traveling in a big circle. Picturing the country in his mind, Kilkenny began to believe they were heading for Cottonwood. But why Cottonwood? Could they by chance know of the wires he had sent? Were they afraid of what those wires might mean to them? Or were they watching the station on orders from the unknown in the cliff house?

On impulse, Kilkenny swung the buckskin from the trail and cut across country for Cottonwood. Now he kept to the cover, and rode steadily by gulch and by cañon, toward the little station.

That night he bedded down on the same creek that ran into Cottonwood, but about six miles upstream from the town. His camp was a dark camp, and he tried no fire, eating a cold supper and falling asleep under the stars.

With daylight he was up. Carefully he cleaned his guns and reloaded them. He knew the Brockmans, and was under no misapprehension as to their skill. They were good, and they were dangerous together. If only by some fortune or stratagem he could catch each one alone. It was a thought, but the two ate together, slept beside each other, walked the streets together, and rode together.

It was almost 9:00 A.M. before he saddled up and rode into town. If his calculations were correct, he was still ahead of the Brockmans. He would still make Cottonwood first, but, if not first, at almost the same time.

When he reached town, he tied Buck under the trees on the edge of the stream, and walked across the little log footbridge to the street. There was nothing much in Cottonwood. On one side of the street was the little stream, never more than six feet wide, and a row of cottonwood trees backed by some bunches of willow beyond the stream. On the opposite side were the telegraph office and station, a bar, a small store, and four or five houses. That was about all. Kilkenny walked into the station.

"Any messages for me?" he asked.

The stationkeeper nodded and stretched. "Yeah. Just come in. Three of 'em."

He passed the messages across to Kilkenny, broke a straw off the broom, and began to chew it slowly and carefully, glancing out the window occasionally.

"Reckon there'll be some fireworks now," he said, nodding at the messages. "It shore beats the devil."

Kilkenny pocketed the messages without glancing at them, left the station, and crossed the street to the willows, after a

98

brief glance into the bar. On the far side of the bridge he lay down on the grass and began to doze.

He was still there an hour later when the stationmaster came to the door. "Hossmen comin' out of the brakes, stranger!" he called out. "They look powerful like the Brockmans!"

Kilkenny got up slowly and stretched. Then he leaned against the trunk of a huge cottonwood. Waiting.

The riders turned into the road leading to Cottonwood at a fast trot. There were three of them now. Kilkenny did not know the third man. They came on at a fast trot. As they reined in suddenly in front of the bar, Kilkenny stepped out and walked across the bridge.

Abel Brockman had swung down. Hearing the footsteps on the bridge, he turned and glanced over his shoulder. His hand stiffened, and he said something, low-voiced, and began to turn. The Brockmans had been caught offside.

Kilkenny stepped out quickly from under the trees. "All right!" he yelled.

Up the street a man sitting on a bench in front of a door suddenly fell backward off the bench and began to scramble madly for the door. Cain Brockman was still in the saddle, but he grabbed for his gun. As Abel's hand moved, Kilkenny's hand whipped down in the lightning draw that had made him famous. His gun came up, steadied, and even as Abel's six-shooter cleared his holster, Kilkenny fired.

Walking toward them he opened up with both guns. Abel got off a shot, but he had been knocked off balance by Kilkenny's first shot, and he staggered into the hitch rail. Cain's horse reared wildly, and the big man toppled backward to the ground. Kilkenny walked on, firing. Abel went to one knee, swung up, lurching, and his guns began to roar again.

Unbelieving, Kilkenny stopped and steadied his hand, then

fired again. He was sure he had hit Abel Brockman with at least four shots.

Abel started to fall, and, swinging on his heel, Kilkenny tried to get a shot at the third man. But, grabbing Cain Brockman, the fellow dragged him around the corner out of sight. One of the horses trotted after them. Gun in hand, Kilkenny walked up to Abel.

Lying on his back in the dust, hand clutching an empty gun, his chest covered with blood, Abel Brockman stared at him.

"Cain'll kill you for this!" he snarled, his eyes burning. "Cain'll . . . oh!" Abel's face twisted with agony. "Cain . . . where's . . . ?"

One hand, thrust up and straining, fell into the dust, and Kilkenny, who had lifted his eyes toward the corner, started toward it.

Then he heard a sudden rattle of hoofs, and he broke into a run.

The third man, whoever he had been, with Cain Brockman across his saddle was taking off up the trail.

Kilkenny stared after them a moment, then shrugged, and walked back. He didn't think he had hit Cain Brockman. Probably he had been thrown from his horse and knocked cold.

Kilkenny retrieved Buck and swung into the saddle. Then he rode back by the station. The stationmaster thrust his head out.

"Didn't think you could do it, mister!" he said. "Some shootin'!"

"Thanks. And thanks for the warnin'." Kilkenny jerked his head back at Abel Brockman's body. "Better get that out of the street. He's pretty big and he'll probably spoil right fast."

He turned Buck toward the Botalla trail, and started down it. Well, it wouldn't be long now. He slapped Buck on the shoulder and lifted his voice in song:

I have a word to speak, boys, only one to say,

Don't never be no cow thief, don't never ride no
  stray.
Be careful of your rope, boys, and keep it on the tree,
But suit yourself about it, for it's nothin' at all to me!

Yet, even as he sang, he was thinking of the problems ahead. It was the time to strike now before anything else was done by the man at Apple Cañon to stir up strife between the Steele and Lord factions. If he and the ranchers and Botalla men could attack Apple Cañon and rout out the rustlers living in the long house there, and either capture them or send them over the border, much of the trouble would be over.

The cowpunchers of the two ranches would still have hard feelings, all too easily aroused if the proper stories were circulated and there should be more killing. Kilkenny realized that. So the thing to do was to strike before the man at the cañon could direct another move. That meant they must move at once—now!

CHAPTER THIRTEEN

Polti was dead. Abel Brockman was dead. That much at least had been done. Cain Brockman was alive. How would he react? Would he come out to kill Kilkenny as Abel had maintained? Would he flee the country, harassed by the thought of his brother's being gone? Would his confidence be ruined? There was no guessing what the man might do, and, despite the death of Abel, Kilkenny knew that Cain Brockman was still a dangerous man. Then two others remained, for Kilkenny was convinced that the unknown killer on the range and the man at Apple Cañon were not one and the same. Two men left, and no hint of who either one was.

On a sudden hunch, Kilkenny turned the buckskin and took a cut-off across the hills toward Apple Cañon. Another talk with Nita might give him some clue. Or was he fooling himself? Was it simply because he wanted to see the hazel-eyed girl who had stirred him so deeply?

He rode on, his face somber, thinking of her. A man who rode the lonely trails had no right to talk love to a woman. What did he have to offer? He had nothing, and always in the background was the knowledge that someday he would be too slow. He couldn't always win. Confident as he was, certain as he was of his skill, he knew that a day must come when he *would* be too slow. Either that, or it would be a shot in the back by an enemy, or a shot from someone who wanted to be able to say he was the man who killed Kilkenny. That was what any gunman of repute had always to fear. For there were many such.

More, there was that curious thing that made gunmen seek each other out to see who was fastest. Men had been known to ride for miles with only that in mind. Sometimes those meetings had come off quietly and without actual shooting. Sometimes it was a matter of mutual respect, as in the case of Wild Bill Hickok and John Wesley Hardin. Some gunmen did live together, some were friends, but they were the exception, and there was always the chance that some ill-considered remark might set off the explosion that might leave a dozen men lying in death.

No, men who lived by the gun died by the gun, and no such man had any right to marry. No matter where he might go in the West, there would always be someone, sometime, who would know him. Then his name would become known again, and he must either fight or be killed. Billy the Kid, Wild Bill, Ben Thompson, King Fisher, Phil Coe, and many another were to prove the old belief in dying by the gun. One day the time would come for him, too, and, until then, his only safety lay in moving on, in being what he had always been, a shadow on the border, a mysterious, little-known gunman who no man could surely describe.

The buckskin skirted the base of a hill, and came out among some cedars. Below lay Apple Cañon.

Thoughtfully Kilkenny studied the town. It seemed quiet, and there was no telltale flash from the cliff house. It might be that he could visit the town without being seen.

Carefully, keeping to cover of the scattered groves of cedar, Kilkenny worked his way along the mountainside, steadily getting closer and closer to the bottom. There was no sign of life.

Finally, close to the foot of the hill, he dismounted and tied the buckskin to a tree with a slipknot. Enough of a tie to let the buckskin know he should stand, but not enough to hold him if

Kilkenny should whistle for him. Then, keeping the saloon between himself and the livery stable, Kilkenny walked casually out of the trees toward the back of the bar.

The biggest chance of being seen would be from the Sadler house, or by someone walking down the short street of the town. He made the trees around Nita's house without being seen. Carefully he placed a hand on the fence, then vaulted it, landing lightly behind the lilacs.

Inside the house someone was singing in a contralto voice, singing carelessly and without pretense as people sing when the song is from the heart more than the brain. It was an old song, a tender song, and for a long time Kilkenny stood there by the lilacs, listening. Then he moved around the bushes and stopped by the open window.

The girl stood there, just inside, almost within the reach of his arm. She had an open book in her hands, but she was not reading. She was looking out at the hills across the valley, out across the roof of the livery stable at the crags.

"It's a lovely picture," he said softly, "a mighty lovely picture. Makes me regret my misspent life."

She did not jump or show surprise, nor at first did her head turn. She kept her eyes on the distant crags, and smiled slowly.

"Strange that you should come now," she said softly. "I had been thinking of you. I was just wondering what you were like as a little boy, what your mother was like, and your father."

Kilkenny took off his hat and leaned on the window sill.

"Does it matter?" he asked softly. "No man is anything but what he is himself. I expect his blood has something to do with it, but not so much. It's what he does with himself, afterward. That's what matters. And I haven't done so well."

"No? I would say, Kilkenny, that you had done well. I would think you are an honorable man."

"I've killed men. Too many."

Rider of Lost Creek

She shrugged. "Perhaps that is bad, but it is the West. I do not believe you ever shot a man from malice, or because there was cruelty in you. Nor do I believe you ever shot one for gain. If you killed, it was because you had to."

"That's the way I wanted it," he said somberly, "but it ain't always been that way. Sometimes you stand in a bar, and you see a man come in, and, when you look at him, you can tell by his eyes and his guns that he's a gunslinger. That's when you should leave. You should get out of there, but you don't, and then sooner or later you have to kill him. You have power when you can sling a gun, but it's an ugly power, and it keeps a man thinkin', worryin' for fear someday he may use it wrong."

"But Kilkenny," Nita said, "surely the West needs good men who can shoot. If there were only the bad men, only the killers, then what chance would honest people have? We need men like you. Oh, I know! Killing is bad, it's wrong. But here in the West men carry guns . . . for wild steers, for rattlesnakes, for Comanches, or rustlers . . . and some learn to use them too well. But the West can't grow without them, Kilkenny."

He looked at her for a long moment. "You're a smart girl, Nita. You think, don't you?"

"Is that good, Kilkenny?" The hazel eyes were soft. "I'm not sure that a girl should ever think, or at least she shouldn't let a man know it."

"That's what they say." He grinned suddenly. "But not for me. I want a girl who can think. I want a girl to walk beside me, not behind me."

"Kilkenny," she said, and her hand suddenly came out to touch his, "be careful! He . . . he's deadly, Kilkenny. He's as vicious as a coiled snake, and he's living just for one thing now . . . to kill you! I don't think it is for the reason he gives. I think it is because he hates you for your reputation! I think he's a little afraid, too. He was drinking once, and he told me, when we were standing at the gate, that he wasn't afraid of Hardin. He said he knew he could beat Hardin or King Fisher. He said in all his life only two men had him bothered. Ben Thompson and you. He's always talking about you when he's drinking. He said Thompson had more nerve than any man he ever knew. And he said that, if you ever fought him, you'd have to be sure he was dead, because if he wasn't and he could walk, he'd come after you again. You bothered him because he said he couldn't place you. You were like a ghost. Nobody could say anything about you except that you were fast and hard-shooting."

Kilkenny nodded. "Yeah, I know what he means. When you're fast with a six-gun, you get to hearin' about others. After a while you get a picture of 'em in your mind, and, when you shoot, you shoot with that picture in mind. Most times you're right, too. But when you don't know about a man, it bothers you. A stranger rides in, wearin' his gun tied down, or mebbe two guns, and he's got a still, cold face, and he drinks with his left hand. Well, you know he's bad. You know he's a gun slick, but you don't know who he is. It leaves you restless and uncertain. Once you know what he is, then you know what you're up against."

They stood there for a while in the warm sun, and a little breeze stirred, and the lilac petals sifted over his shoulders, and he could smell their heavy perfume. He looked up at the girl and felt a strange yearning rise within him. It wasn't merely the yearning of a man for a woman. It was the longing of a man for a home, for a fireside, for the laughter of children, and the quiet of night with someone lying beside you. The yearning for someone to work for, to protect, someone to belong to, and some place in life where you fitted in.

It was so different from all he had known these last bitter years. These years of endless watchfulness, of continual awareness, of looking into each man's eyes, and wondering if he was another man you would have to kill, of riding down long trails, always aware that a bullet might cut you down. Yet, even as he thought of that, he knew there was something in his blood that answered to the wild call of the wilderness trails. There was something about riding into a strange town, swinging down from his horse, and walking into a bar, something that gave him a lift, and that gave life a strange zest.

There was something in the pounding of guns, the buck of a .45 in his hand, the leap of a horse beneath him, and the shouts of men, something that awakened everything that was in him. Times bred the men they needed, and the West needed such men, men who could bring peace to a strange, wild land, even while they found death for themselves. The West was won by gunmen no less than it was won by pioneering families, by fur traders and Indian fighters.

"What are you going to do, Kilkenny, when all this is over?" Nita asked softly.

He leaned his elbows on the window sill and pushed his hat back on his head. "I don't rightly know," he said thoughtfully. "I reckon I'll just move on to some other town. Might rustle me a herd of cows and settle down somewheres on a piece of land. Mebbe over in the Big Bend country."

"Why don't you marry and have a home, Kilkenny?" Nita asked softly. "I think you'd make a good man around a home."

"Me?" He laughed, a bit harshly. "All I can do is sling a gun. That ain't much good around a house. Of course, I might punch cows, or play poker?" He straightened suddenly. "Time I was ridin' on. You be careful." Then he paused. "Tell me, Nita. What hold does this man have over you?"

"None. It is as I have said. I like to live, even here, and alone. I know I would die, and quickly, if I talked. Then, after a fashion, he has protected me. Of course, *señor*"—she fell into her old way of speaking—"it is that he wants me for himself. But I belong to no man. Yet."

"You can't tell me who he is?"

"No." She looked at him for a minute. "Perhaps you think I am not helping, but, you see, this is all I have, this place. When it is gone, there is nothing. And the people out there"—she waved a hand toward Botalla—"do not think I am good. There would be no place for me there. I can only say that he will kill you if he can, and you must be careful if you go to the cliff. And do not go by the path."

When he was back on the buckskin, he turned toward Botalla. If Steele and Lord had their men there, he would bring them back to Apple Cañon at once. In his ride to the place he had carefully scouted the approaches.

It had been easy enough to see just what they would be facing in an attack on the stronghold. He could muster about sixty men. There would be at least forty here at the cañon. Sixty wasn't really enough, for the men at the cañon would be fighting on their own ground, and behind defenses. And all were seasoned fighters. Nevertheless, much could be lost by waiting. The time was now. The raid on Apple Cañon, however, might leave the range killer at large.

As Kilkenny rode, his brain dug into the accumulated evidence, little as it was. Yet one idea refused to be denied, and it worried around in his mind until he reached town.

He came up to the Trail House at a spanking trot. Dropping from saddle, he flipped a dollar to a Mexican boy.

"Take that horse, Pedro," he said, grinning, "and treat him right. Oats, hay, water, and a rub-down."

Pedro dropped his bare feet to the boardwalk and grinned, showing his white teeth.

"*Sí, señor*, it shall be done!"

Chapter Fourteen

Rusty Gates was sitting inside the Trail House, holding himself stiffly, but grinning. Webb Steele was there, too. He looked up keenly as Kilkenny came in.

"Can't keep a good man down!" Rusty said. "Tana bandaged my side, and I wanted to give you a hand with the Brockmans, but she wouldn't let me. She's got a mind of her own, that girl!"

"What happened?" Frame demanded, stepping up.

"Got Abel," said Kilkenny. "Cain got thrown from his horse. Knocked out, I think. Another *hombre* dragged him around a corner and got him aboard a horse. They lit out, and I let 'em go."

Frame shook his head, his eyes dark with worry. "Cain will go crazy when he finds out Abel is dead and you're still alive. He'll come gunnin' for you, Kilkenny."

"He might." Kilkenny shrugged. "Got to take that chance. We're after bigger game now. We've got to wipe out that bunch at Apple Cañon. There's at least forty outlaws there."

"Probably more," Steele said. "Clyde Wilder was down there a few days ago, and he says there was anyways fifty, and might have been seventy."

"Don't make no difference," Frame declared. "We're ready. Even Duval at the hotel is goin'. Everybody wants to lend a hand."

Down the main street of Botalla there was suddenly a pound-

ing of hoofs, then a rider threw himself from saddle in front of
the Trail House. He thrust the batwing doors open with his
shoulder.

"Kilkenny!" he yelled. "Chet Lord's dyin'! Wants to see you,
the worst way!"

"What happened?" Steele demanded.

"Gored by a crazy steer. Don't reckon he's got long. Askin'
for Kilkenny. Don't know what he wants of him."

"Steele," Kilkenny said, "get the men together, plenty of
arms an' ammunition. Nobody leaves town to warn Apple
Cañon. Get set to move, and, when you're ready, start her
rollin'!"

He swung into saddle and turned the buckskin toward the
Lord Ranch. His mind was working swiftly. What could Chet
Lord have to say? That something had been worrying the big
rancher for days was obvious enough, for the man had lost
weight, he looked drawn and pale, and seemed to be under
great strain.

Was he the unknown killer? As soon as that idea occurred,
Kilkenny shook his head. The man was not the type. Bluff,
outspoken, and direct, he was the kind of man who would shoot
straight and die hard, but his shots would be at a man's face,
not behind his back.

Kilkenny let the buckskin take his own gait. The long-legged
horse knew his rider, and knew the mountains and desert. He
knew that on many days he would be called on for long, hard
rides, and had learned to pace himself accordingly. While cow
ponies were held in light esteem, good as they might be, by
most cowpunchers who also might have their favorites, it was
the gunmen and outlaws, the men whose lives might depend on
the horses they rode, who really knew and cared for their horses.
It was a time when a few such horses were to acquire almost as
much fame as their hard-riding, straight-shooting masters. Sam

Bass, for instance, was to become no more famous than the Denton mare he rode. And Black Nell, Wild Bill Hickok's horse with a trick of "dropping quick", was to save Hickok's life on more than one occasion. Kilkenny knew his buckskin, and Buck knew Kilkenny. During the years they had been together, they had learned each other's ways, and Buck had almost human intelligence when it came to knowing what his master wanted of him. He knew the ways of the frontier, and seemed to sense when there he could husband his strength, and when it must be used. Buck's ears were as perfect a guide to danger as a rifle shot. A flicker of movement, even miles ahead, and his ears were up and alert. And when he side-stepped, it was always with reason.

The Lord Ranch was strangely still when the buckskin cantered across the yard and came to a stop before the ranch house. Kilkenny swung to the ground and, leaving Buck ground-hitched, went up the steps at a bound.

Steve met him at the door. The young fellow's eyes were wet, and his face looked pale.

"He wants you," he said. "Wants you bad."

Kilkenny stepped through the door into the room where Chet Lord lay in bed. A sharp-eyed man with a beard stood up when Kilkenny walked in.

"I'm Doc Wentlow," he said softly, then smiled a little wryly. "From Apple Cañon. He wants to talk to you"—he glanced at Steve—"alone."

"Right."

The doctor and Steve went out, and Kilkenny watched them go. He saw Steve hesitate in the door as though loath to leave. Then the young cowboy stepped out, and Kilkenny turned to the old man lying on the bed. Lord's breathing was heavy, but his eyes were open. His face seemed to have aged, and he looked

111

up at Kilkenny for a moment, then reached over and took his hand.

"Kilkenny," he whispered hoarsely, "I got a favor to ask. You got to promise me, for I'm a dyin' man. Promise me you'll do it. It's somethin' you can do."

"Shore," Kilkenny said gently. "If it's anything I can do, I will. You know that."

"Kilkenny," the old man's voice faltered, then his grip tightened on Kilkenny's wrist until the gun expert almost winced with the strength of it, "Kilkenny, I want you to kill my son."

"What?" Kilkenny stared. Then his eyes narrowed slowly. "Why, Lord?"

"Kilkenny, you got to. Kilkenny, I'm an old man, and, wrong or right, I love my boy. I love him like I loved his mother before him, but, Kilkenny, he's a killer! He's insane! I've knowed it for months now! Des told me. Des King told me before Steve killed him. Long time ago, Steve had a bad fall off a buckin' hoss, and was unconscious for days and days. He was kind of queer when he got well, for a spell, then it looked like he was all right again, and didn't take pleasure in torturin' things no more. So when folks began to get killed around here, I never thought of the boy. Then I had a feelin', and one day Des come to me, and said he knowed Steve had done it, and that he'd have to be put away. He couldn't go on killin' folks. But then Des was killed, an' I couldn't bear to put Steve away. He . . . he . . . was all . . . I had, Kilkenny."

Kilkenny nodded slowly, looking down at the old man, seeing the pleading in his eyes, the plea for understanding, for sympathy at least.

"I done wrong. I knowed I was doin' wrong, but I hoped the boy would change. Sometimes he would be a good boy, then he'd get to moonin' around, then off he'd go."

For a long time the old man was silent, then his chest heaved and he turned his head.

"Kilkenny, you got to kill him. I won't be around no more to look after him, and you'll kill him decent, Kilkenny. You'll shoot him, and he won't suffer. I don't want him to suffer, Kilkenny. He's a baby for pain. He can't suffer. I don't want him hung, neither, Kilkenny. Go shoot him down. I left a paper. It's in a envelope, in case I die. Frame has got it. It tells all about it. Kilkenny, you got to kill him. I can't die thinkin' I've left that passel of evil behind me. An' but for that, he's been a good boy."

Kilkenny still stood staring down at old Chet Lord. Yes, it all fitted. Everything fitted. Steve had a Winchester 1873, and he could have done any of the shootings. Kilkenny had suspected something of the kind, which was why he had wired.

Wired?

Kilkenny clapped a hand to his pocket. Why, the wires! He'd had them in his pocket all the time! Hurriedly he dug into his pocket and pulled them out, unfolding the sheets.

The first was from San Antonio, and it was a verification of what Chet Lord had just told him, a few scattered facts about Steve's boyhood actions after his bucking horse accident, before his father had taken him away, all indicative of what might later come. That was unnecessary now. There would be evidence enough. His father's letter with Frame, and a few dates and times would piece it all together.

He unfolded the second message, from El Paso. As its message struck him, his hands stiffened.

TYSON SAW ROYAL BARNES AT APPLE CAÑON. HE KNEW BARNES FROM HAYS CITY AND ABI-LENE. BARNES MURDERED TYSON'S BROTHER, AND HE HEARD BARNES SWEAR TO KILL YOU FOR GETTING THE WEBERS. BE CAREFUL, KILKENNY,

HE'S COLD AS A SNAKE, AND LIGHTNING FAST.

Kilkenny crumpled the message into a ball and thrust it into his pocket. The third message no longer mattered. It had only been an effort to learn what gunslingers were where, in an effort to learn who was at Apple Cañon. Now he knew.

Royal Barnes! The name stood out boldly in his mind, and, even as he turned away from the old man on the bed, he saw that name, the name of a man he had never seen, the name of one of the most ruthless, cold-blooded killers in the West. A man as evil and vicious as any, yet reputed to be handsome, reputed to be smooth and polished, yet known to be a man filled with the lust to kill and of such deadly skill that it was said that Wes Hardin had backed down for him.

Kilkenny opened the door and stepped outside. Instantly Doc Wentlow got up.

"How is he?" he demanded.

"Pretty low." Kilkenny hesitated. "Where's Steve?"

"Steve? That was funny. He stood by the door a minute after you went in. Listening, I guess. Then all of a sudden he turned and got on a horse and took off, riding like the devil."

Despite himself, Kilkenny felt relieved. He had never killed a man unless the man was attempting to kill him. To walk out of the old cattleman's bed chamber and shoot Steve had been the furthest from his thoughts. Just what he had hoped to do, he was not sure. He did know that Steve Lord must be stopped.

Thinking back, he could remember the curious light, the blazing of some inner compulsion, which he had seen in Steve's eyes that first day in the Trail House. Yet Steve had not wanted to shoot it out with him, face to face. The young fellow was a man with an insane urge to kill. It grew from some inner feeling of inferiority. What Steve Lord would do now, Kilkenny could not guess. He knew killers, but the killers he knew were sane men, men whose thoughts could be read, and whose ways could be known. He did know that even the craziest man had his moments of sanity, and he knew that Steve Lord must have listened at the door, probably suspecting what his father intended to tell Kilkenny. So he had mounted and ridden away—to what? Where could he go? Yet even as the question came, he knew its answer. Steve Lord would go to Apple Cañon.

However insane the boy might be, there was some connection between him and the events stemming from the cañon rendezvous. And Kilkenny suspected that Steve had more than a little interest in Nita Riordan. But he would be riding now with fear in his heart, with desperation. For now he was in the open, the place he dreaded to be, where there was no concealment. He must fight, or he must die, and Kilkenny knew that such a man would fight like a cornered rat. Yet he had promised a dying man, and regardless of that it was something that had to be done.

Why should he feel depressed? Steve was a killer, preying upon the lonely and the helpless, a man who shot from ambush, who killed from sheer love of killing. So he must be stopped. It was his own father, the man who sired him, who had passed sentence upon him.

Kilkenny turned off into the thick brush, unrolled his poncho, and was asleep almost as soon as he lay down.

CHAPTER FIFTEEN

Botalla's Main Street was crowded with horsemen when Kilkenny rode back to the town. They were in for the finish, the lean, hard-bitten, wind- and gun-seasoned veterans of the Texas range. Riders from the Steele and Lord Ranches, men who had ridden the long cattle trails north to Dodge and Abilene, men who knew the ways of cows and Indians and guns. Men who had cut their teeth on six-shooters.

Yet, as Kilkenny rode up the street, eyes alert for some sign of Steve Lord, he wondered how many of these men would be alive when another sundown came. For they were facing men as tough as themselves, as good, and as dangerous as cornered rats are always dangerous. Vicious as men can be who find themselves faced at last with justice and the necessity of paying for their misdeeds. They would fight, shrewdly and well. They were not common criminals, these men of Apple Cañon. A few, yes. But many were just tough young men who had taken the wrong trail or liked the hard, reckless life. A different turn of events and they might have been satisfied cowhands, trail bosses, or they might have been Rangers. They would ask no quarter, and they would give none. They would fight this out to the last bitter ditch, and they would go down, guns blazing. They might have taken the wrong trails, but they had courage.

And for him? There was none of that; there was just one man. He had to mount that cliff and take Royal Barnes, the mysterious man in the cliff house. How would he know him?

He did not know, but he did know that when he saw the man he would know him. Instinctively he knew that. When a man looked at another across a space of ground, with guns waiting, then he knew whether a man was fast and whether he would kill or not.

This would be different. Lance Kilkenny understood that. The Brockmans had been good but he had timed his chances to nullify their skill as a twin fighting combination. He had killed Abel Brockman as he had killed many another man, and most of them fast. But—and this he knew—he had never drawn against a man like Royal Barnes. Blinding speed. Barnes had that. Barnes had killed Blackie Slade, and Kilkenny recalled Slade only too well. He had seen Slade in action, and the man had been poison. Yet Barnes had shot him down as if he were an amateur.

Yet Kilkenny could feel something building up inside himself, and recognized what it was. It was his own compulsion, his own fire to kill. Every gunman had it. Without it, he was helpless. It was a fiery drive, but with it the cold ruthlessness of a man who knew he must kill, or he must die himself.

He swung down from his horse and walked into the Trail House.

"We're all set," Webb Steele said, walking forward. "All set, and roarin' to go. The boys wanted to wait and see how Chet is."

Kilkenny looked up. "Steele," he said slowly, "Chet's dyin'. He told me about the killin's. It's Steve. Steve's a killer!"

Webb Steele stared, and Frame rubbed the back of his hand across his eyes.

"Huh!" Steele said. "I might've knowed it! He was always a strange 'un."

"That ain't all," Kilkenny said quietly. "The man up in the cliff house is Royal Barnes."

"Barnes?" Rusty Gates's face tightened, then turned gray as he looked at Kilkenny. "One of the slickest *hombres* that ever threw a six-gun."

In the stillness that followed men stared at one another and into the mind of each came stories they had heard of Royal Barnes and of the men who had gone down before his roaring guns. In the mind of each was a fear that he might be next.

The silence was shattered by the crashing of a door, and as one man the crowd turned to stare at the rear door of the Trail House. Several steps inside that door, his head thrust forward and his eyes glaring with killing hatred, stood a huge, broad-jawed man in a checked shirt and black jeans stuffed into heavy cowhide boots.

"Cain Brockman!" Frame yelled.

The big man strode forward until he stood only three paces from Kilkenny. Then, with cold, merciless hatred in his eyes, he unbuckled his belt and shed his guns.

"I'm goin' to kill you, Kilkenny! With my bare hands!"

"No!" Webb burst out, thrusting himself forward. "We got us a job to do, Kilkenny!"

"Keep out of this," Kilkenny said quietly.

Without further word and without taking his eyes from Cain's, he unbuckled his own belt and passed his guns to the big rancher.

With a hoarse grunt, Cain Brockman lunged, swinging a ponderous right fist. Kilkenny stepped inside and snapped a lightning left to the face, then closed with the big man, slamming both fists to his midriff. Cain grabbed Kilkenny and hurled him across the room so that he brought up with a crash against the bar. Cain lunged after him.

Kilkenny pivoted away, stabbing a left that caught the bigger man on the cheek bone, then Brockman swung and caught Kilkenny with a hard right swing that knocked him to his knees.

A kick aimed at Kilkenny's shoulder just grazed him as he was starting to rise. He lost balance, toppling over on the floor. He rolled away and came up swinging, and the two sprang together.

Brockman's face was savage with killing fury and an ugly glee at having his enemy and the man who had slain his brother actually in his hands. Another right caught Kilkenny a glancing blow, but he weathered it and stepped under a left, slamming a right to the ribs. Then he hooked a left to the chin, leaping away before Cain could grab him.

It was toe-to-toe, slam-bang fighting, and neither man was taking any precaution. Both fought like savages, and Kilkenny's face became set in a mask of fierce desperation as he met charge after charge of the huge Brockman. They stood, straddle-legged, in the middle of the floor and swung until the smacking sound of their blows sounded loudly in the room and blood streamed from cut and battered faces. Brockman was a brute for strength, and he was out for a kill, filled with so much fury that he was almost immune to pain.

Kilkenny stepped inside a right and ripped his own right to the heart. He hooked both hands to the body, then they grappled and went to the floor, kicking and gouging. There were no rules here, no niceties of combat. This was fighting to maim, to kill, and there was only one possible end—the finish of one or the other.

Blood streaming from a cut on his cheek, Kilkenny lanced a left to the mouth, then missed a right and took a wicked left to the middle. But he took the punch going in, punching with both hands to the head.

Cain's big head rocked with the force of the blows and he spat a tooth onto the floor, and swung hard to the head, staggering Kilkenny. The gunman came back fast, ripping a right uppercut to the chin, then a left and right to the head. Kilkenny was boxing now. Long ago he had taken lessons from one of the

119

best fighters of the day, and he found now that he needed every bit of his skill.

It was not merely a matter of defeating Cain Brockman. After that, and perhaps soon, he would be meeting Royal Barnes, and his hands must be strong and ready. He stepped inside of a right and smashed a right to the bigger man's body, then hooked a left to the heart, and drummed with both hands against the big man's torso. Body punches stood less chance of hurting his hands, and he must be careful.

He stepped around, putting Brockman off side, and then crossed a right to Cain's bleeding eye, circled farther left, and crossed the right again. Then he stabbed three lefts to the face, and, as Cain lunged, he stepped inside and butted him under the chin with his head.

Brockman let out a muffled roar and crowded Kilkenny to the bar, but Lance wormed away and slugged the big man in the ribs. Brockman was slowing down now, and his face was bloody and swollen. His eyes gleamed fiercely, and he began to move slowly, more cautiously, watching for his chance. Brockman backed up, backed slowly, trying to keep away from that stabbing left, then suddenly he brought up against the wall. Putting a foot against the wall, he shoved himself off it like a huge battering ram and caught Kilkenny fully in the chest with his big head. Kilkenny went crashing to the floor!

Brockman rushed close, trying to kick him in the ribs, but Kilkenny got to his hands and knees and hurled himself against Brockman's legs. The big man tumbled over him, then spun on the floor with amazing agility and grabbed Kilkenny's head, groping for his eyeballs with his thumbs!

Mad with pain and fear for his eyes, Kilkenny tore loose and lunged to his feet. Brockman came up with him and Kilkenny stabbed a powerful left into that wide granite-hard face. Blood flew in every direction, and he felt the nose bone crunch under his fist. With a cry of pain, Cain Brockman lunged forward, and his mighty blows pounded at Kilkenny's body. But the lighter man blocked swiftly and caught most of the blows on his elbows and shoulders. Driven back, the gun expert swayed like a tree in a gale, fighting desperately to set himself, to stave off that terrific assault. There was the taste of blood in his mouth and he felt his lungs gasping for breath, and their gasping was a tearing pain.

Brockman closed in and thrust out a left that might have ended the fight, but Kilkenny went under it and butted Cain in the chest, staggering the bigger man. Missing a right hook to the head, Kilkenny split Brockman's cheek wide open with his elbow, ripped the elbow back, slamming the big man's head around.

Despite the fierceness of the fighting, Kilkenny was not badly hurt. Most of the bigger man's blows had been wasted. One eye was cut, and he knew his jaw was swollen, but mainly he was fighting to stave off the big man's fierce attacks. They swept forward with tremendous power, but little skill. Yet Kilkenny was growing desperate. His punches seemed to have no effect on the huge hulk of Cain Brockman. The big man's face was bleeding from several cuts. His lips were battered, and one eye was badly swollen, but he seemed to have got his second wind, and was no less strong than when he had thrown his first punch. On his part, Kilkenny had one eye almost swollen shut. He could taste blood from a cut inside his mouth, and his breath was coming in those tearing gasps.

Brockman bored in, swinging. Kilkenny pushed the left swing outward and stepped in, bringing up a hard left uppercut to the wind that stopped Brockman in his tracks. But the big man bowed his head and lunged. Kilkenny dropped an open palm to the head and shoved the fellow off balance, and, as his guard came down for an instant, he stabbed a left to Brockman's cut eye. Then he circled warily.

Cain lunged, kicked at Kilkenny's middle. The lighter man jerked back, then stepped off to the left, and dived in a long flying tackle. He hit Brockman at the knees, grabbed, and jerked hard! Brockman came down with a thud, his head bouncing on the wood floor. Kilkenny rolled free and scrambled to his feet. Brockman was getting up, but he was slow. Half up, he lunged in a long dive himself, but Kilkenny jerked his knee into the big man's face. Cain rolled off to one side, his face bloody and scarcely human. Yet even then he tried to get up.

He made it. Kilkenny was sick of the fight, sick of the beating he was giving the bigger man. He stepped in, measured him with a left, and, when Cain tried to lift his hands, Kilkenny slugged him in the solar plexus. The big man went down, conscious, but paralyzed from the waist down.

Kilkenny stepped back, weaving with exhaustion. Grimly he worked his battered, stiffened hands.

"You ain't in shape for that raid now, Kilkenny," Rusty expostulated. "Better call it off or stay behind."

"To thunder with that," Kilkenny replied sharply. "I want Royal Barnes myself, and I'll get him."

Walking back to the wash basin, he dipped up water from the bucket and bathed his cut and bruised face. He turned his head as Frame walked up, his face grave.

"Get me some salts," Kilkenny said.

While he waited, he bathed his hands and replaced his torn shirt with one brought him by Gates.

When he had the salts, he put them in hot water one of the men brought and soaked them. He knew there was nothing better for taking away soreness and stiffness, and it was only his hands he was worried about. He was bruised and battered, but not seriously. Although that one eye was swollen, he could still see through the slit.

Finally he straightened. He turned and looked at the men around him. They would never ride without him, he knew, or, if they did, their hearts wouldn't be in it. He laughed suddenly.

"All-l-l set!" he yelled. "Let's ride!"

Chapter Sixteen

On Buck, Kilkenny headed toward the Apple Cañon trail. He was tired, his muscles were weary and heavy, yet he knew that the outdoor life he had lived, and the rugged existence he had known most of his life would give him the stamina he needed now. Behind him a tight cavalcade of grim, mounted men were riding out to battle.

Rusty Gates rode up alongside Kilkenny in the van of the column.

"You had yourself a scrap," Rusty said. "Can you see?"

"Enough."

"How about your hands?" Gates noticed the swollen knuckles and his lips tightened. "Kilkenny, you can't drag a fast gun with hands like that. Facin' Barnes will be suicide."

"Nevertheless, I'm facin' him," Kilkenny said crisply. "He's my meat, and I'll take him. Besides, my hands ain't as bad as they look, and most of that swelling will be gone soon. It ain't goin' to be speed that'll win, anyway. Both of us are goin' to catch lead. It'll be who can take the most of it and keep goin'." He nodded. "The way I figure it we'll be spotted before we get there. They'll be holed up around the buildin's. The bunkhouse, the livery stable, and blacksmith shop all looked like they was built to stand a siege."

"They were," said Rusty. "Heavy logs or stone, and built solid. Bill Sadler's place, on the same side as the Border Bar, is 'dobe, and it has walls three feet thick. Them windows was built to cover the trail, an' believe me, it ain't a goin' to be no picnic gettin' tough men out of there."

"I know." Kilkenny rubbed Buck's neck thoughtfully. "Got to figger that one out. I'm thinkin' of leavin' you fellers anyway. I'm goin' up to the castle."

"Alone?" Gates was incredulous. "Man, you're askin' for it. He'll be forted up there, and plenty tight."

"I doubt it. I doubt if he ever lets more than one man up there with him. Royal Barnes, as I hear of him, ain't a trustin' soul. No, I'm goin' to try comin' down the cliffs above the castle."

"The what?" Gates swore and spat into the road. "Holy snakes, feller! They're sheer rock! You'd need a rope and a lot of luck. Then he'd see you and get you before you ever got down!"

"Mebbe, I got the rope, and mebbe the luck. Anyway, I'm comin' down from behind where he won't be expectin' me, an' I'm comin' down while you fellers are hard at it in front. Now here . . . the way I see it. . . ."

As Webb Steele, Frame, and Rusty listened, he outlined a brief plan of attack. At the end, they began to grin.

"Might work," observed Steele. "I'd forgot that claim up in the pass. If that stuff is still there. . . ."

"It is. I looked."

Kilkenny had no illusions about the task ahead. With the plan he had conceived, carefully working it out during the previous days, he believed that the fort houses of Apple Cañon could be taken. It meant a struggle, and there would be loss of life. This riding column would lose some faces, and there would be hectic and bloody fighting before that return.

Where was Steve Lord? Had Steve risen to his bait and ridden to the hidden cabin in the box cañon? It would be a place to find him, and there, if Steve should go for a gun, he could end it all. Kilkenny shrank from the task, and only the

Louis L'Amour

knowledge that other people would die, brutally murdered from ambush, made him willing to go through with keeping his promise to old Chet Lord. He had that job to do, and luckily the cañon was only a short distance from the route the cavalcade would follow.

There had been no diary left by Des King. The idea had been created in Kilkenny's own mind. It had been bait dropped for the killer, and it had been conceived even before Kilkenny had known that Steve was the man. That he would have discovered it soon, he knew, for slowly the evidence had been mounting, and he had been suspicious of Steve Lord, waiting only for a chance to inspect his guns and check them against the shells he had picked up as evidence.

What would Steve Lord do now? To all intents, he would be outlawed. He knew his father had exposed him, and he must realize there was evidence enough to convict him, or to send him to an asylum. He would be desperate. Would he try to kill Kilkenny? To escape? Or would he go on a killing spree and gun down everything and everybody in sight? Kilkenny couldn't escape the feeling that Steve would go to Apple Cañon. He turned suddenly to Webb Steele.

"I'm ridin' for the shack where I let Steve think Des King hid his diary," he said. "If I ain't back when you get to Apple Cañon, just go to work and don't wait for me. I'm goin' to get Steve Lord. When I find him, I'll come back."

He wheeled the buckskin and took off up a draw into the deeper hills. He had been thinking of this route all the way along. He wasn't sure this route would do it, but knew he could find a way.

The draw opened into a narrower draw, and after a long time he rode out of that to a little stretch of bunch grass that led away to a ridge covered with cedar and pine. It was cool among the trees, and he stopped for a minute to wipe his hatband and check his guns once more. Then he slid his Winchester from the scabbard and took it across the saddle in front if him. His hands felt better than he had expected they would.

He struck a path and followed it through the trees, winding steadily upward. Then the trees thinned, and he entered a region of heaped-up boulders among which the trail wound with all the casualness of cow trails in a country where cows are in no hurry. Twice rabbits jumped up and ran away from his trail, but the buckskin's hoofs made no noise on the pine needles or in the dust of the boulder-bordered trail.

Kilkenny was cutting across a meadow when he saw the prints of a horse bisecting the trail he was making. In the tall grass of the meadow he could tell nothing of the horse, but on a hunch he turned the buckskin and followed. Whoever the rider was, he was in a hurry, and was moving in as straight a line as possible for his objective.

It had bad features, this trailing of a man native to the country. Such a man would know of routes, of places of concealment of which Kilkenny could know nothing. Such an advantage could mean the difference between life and death in such a country.

Scanning every open space before he moved across it, Kilkenny followed warily. He knew only too well the small amount of concealment it required to prevent a man from being seen. A few inches of grass, clothes that blended with surroundings, and immobility was all that was essential to remain unseen.

Sunlight caught the highest pinnacles of the mountains beyond Forgotten Pass, and slowly the long shadows crept up, and the day crept away down the cañons. Kilkenny rode steadily, every sense alert for trouble, his keen eyes searching the rocks ahead, roving ceaselessly, warily.

The cabin was not far away when he dismounted and faded into the darkness under the gnarled cedars, and looked down through the narrow entrance between the cliffs into the box cañon.

A squat, shapeless structure, built hurriedly by some wandering prospector or hopeful rancher in some distant period. Then in the years that followed it had slowly sagged here and there, the straw roof rotting and being patched with cedar bows, earth, and even heavy branches from the cedars until the roof had become a mound. It was an ancient, decrepit structure, its one window a black hole, its door too low for a tall man. About it the grass was green, for there was a stream nearby that flowed out of the rocks on one side and returned into the cliffs on the other, after diagonally crossing the cañon and watering a meadow in transit.

Outside the shack, under an apple tree, stood a saddled horse, his head hanging.

Well, here we are, Kilkenny, he told himself dryly. *Now to get close.*

Leaving the buckskin in concealment, Kilkenny went at a crouching run to the nearest boulder. Then he ran closer, crouched behind some cedars, watching the cabin.

He was puzzled. There was still no movement. It should take no time to find there was nothing in the cabin, and it was black in there. He should have seen a light by now, for there was no use trying to search in the blackness inside that cabin for anything.

The saddled horse stood, his head low, waiting wearily. A breeze stirred leaves on the cottonwood tree, and they whispered gently. Kilkenny pulled his sombrero lower and, moving carefully with the whispering of the leaves to cover the rustle of his movement, worked along the cliff into the bottleneck entrance. Slowly, carefully he worked inside.

There was no shot, no sound. In dead silence he moved closer, his rifle ready, his eyes searching every particle of cover.

The horse moved a little, and began cropping grass absently, as though it had already eaten its fill.

Suddenly he had a feeling that the cabin was empty. There was no reason for him to wait. He would go over to it. He stepped out, his rifle ready, and walked swiftly and silently across the grass toward the cabin.

The horse stopped cropping grass and looked up, pricking its ears at him. Then he stepped up to the cabin.

Was there anyone inside? The blackness of the squat cabin gave off no sound. Despite himself, Kilkenny felt uneasy. It was too still, and there was something unearthly about this lost cañon and the lonely little shack. Carefully he put down his rifle and slipped a six-gun into his hand. The rifle would be a handicap if he had to fight in the close quarters of the shack. Then he looked in.

It was black inside, yet between himself and the hole that passed for a window he could see the vague outline of a sleeping man's head. A man's head bowed forward on his chest.

"All right," he said clearly. "You can get up and come out!"

There was neither sound nor movement. Kilkenny stepped inside quickly, and there was still no move. Taking a chance, he struck a match. The man was dead.

Searching about, he found a stump of candle that some passing rider had left. Lighting it, he looked at the man. He was a stranger. A middle-aged man, and a cowhand by his looks. He had been shot in the right temple by someone who had fired from outside the window. The room had been thoroughly ransacked.

Kilkenny scowled. An innocent man killed, and his fault. If he hadn't told that story, this might not have happened. But at the time he had needed some way for the killer to betray himself. It wasn't easy to do everything right.

He walked out quickly and swung into saddle. There was

nothing to do now but to return. He could make it in time, and morning would be the time to attack. In the small hours, just before daylight.

Buck took the trail with a quickened step as though he understood an end was in sight. Kilkenny lounged in the saddle. Steve would be riding hard now. He would be heading for Apple Cañon.

Weary from the long riding and the fight with Cain Brockman, Kilkenny lounged in the saddle, more asleep than awake. The yellow horse ambled down the trail through the mountains like a ghost horse on a mysterious mission.

There was a faint light in the sky, the barest hint of approaching dawn, when Kilkenny rode up to join the posse. They had stopped in a shallow valley about two miles from Apple Cañon. Dismounted, aside from guards, they were gathered about the fire.

He swung down from his horse and walked over, his boots sinking into the sand of the wash. The firelight glowed on their hard, unshaven faces.

Webb Steele, his huge body looking big as a grizzly's, looked up.

"Find Steve?" he demanded.

"No. But he killed another man." Briefly Kilkenny told of what he had found at the cabin. "Steve's obviously come on here. He's somewhere in there."

"You think he worked with this gang?" Frame asked. "Against his own pa?"

"Uhn-huh. I think he knows Barnes. I think they cooked up some kind of a deal. I think Steve Lord has a heavy leanin' toward Nita Riordan, too. That's mebbe why he come here."

Rusty said nothing. He was looking pale, and Kilkenny could see that the ride had been hard on him. He shouldn't have come with that wound, Kilkenny thought. But men like Rusty

Gates couldn't stay out of a good fight. And wounded or not, he was worth any two ordinary men.

Not two like Webb Steele, though. Or Frame. Either of them would do to ride the river with. They might be bull-headed, they might argue and talk a lot, but they were men who believed in doing the right thing, and men who would fight in order to be able to do it.

CHAPTER SEVENTEEN

Glancing around at the others, Kilkenny saw that they looked efficient and sure. All of those men had been through the mill. There probably wasn't a man in the lot who hadn't fought Comanches and rustlers. This was going to be tough, because they were fighting clever men who would kill, and who were fighting from concealment. It is one thing to fight skilled fighting men, who know Indian tactics, and to fight those who battle in the open.

"Well," Kilkenny said, as he tasted the hot, bitter black coffee, "we got to be movin'. The stars are fadin' out a little."

Webb Steele turned to the men.

"You all know what this is about," he said harshly. "We ain't plannin' on no prisoners. Every man who wants to surrender will get his chance. If a man throws down his shootin' iron, take him. We'll try 'em decent, and hang the guilty ones. Although," he added, "ain't likely to be any innocent ones in Apple Cañon."

"One thing," Kilkenny said suddenly. "Leave Nita Riordan's Border Bar and her house alone."

He wasn't sure how they would take that, and he stood there, looking around. He saw tacit approval in Rusty's eyes, and Steele and Frame nodded agreement. Then his eyes encountered those of a tall, lean man with a cadaverous face and piercing gray eyes. The man chewed for a minute in silence, staring at Kilkenny.

"I reckon," he said then harshly, "that if we clear the bad

'uns out of Apple, we better clear 'em all out. Me, I ain't stoppin' for no woman. Nor that half-breed man of her'n, neither!"

Steele's hand tightened, and his eyes narrowed. Kilkenny noticed tension among the crowd. Would there be a split here? He smiled. "No reason for any trouble," he said quietly, "but Nita Riordan gave me a tip once that helped. I think she's friendly to us, an' I think she's innocent of wrongdoin'."

The man with the gray eyes looked back at him. "I aim to clear her out of there as well's the others. I aim to burn that bar over her head."

There was cruelty in the man's face, and a harshness that seemed to spring from some inner source of malice and hatred. He wore a gun tied down, and had a carbine in the hollow of his arm. Several other men had moved up behind him now, and there was a curious similarity in their faces.

"Time to settle that," Kilkenny said, "when we get there. But I'm thinkin', friend, you better change your mind. If you don't, you're goin' to have to kill me along with her."

"She's a scarlet woman," the man said viciously, "and dyin's too good for her kind. I'm a-gettin' her, and you stay away."

"Time's a-wastin'," Steele said suddenly. "Let's ride!"

In the saddle, Kilkenny swung alongside of Steele in the van of the column.

"Who is that *hombre?*" he demanded.

"Name of Calkins. Lem Calkins. He hails from West Virginia . . . lives up yonder in the mountains. He's a feuder. You see them around him? He's got three brothers, and five sons. If you touch one of 'em, you got to fight 'em all."

They rode up the rise before coming to Apple Cañon, and then Kilkenny wheeled his horse toward the cliff. Almost instantly a shot rang out, and he wheeled the buckskin again and went racing toward the street of the town.

More shots rang out, and a man at the well dropped the

bucket and grabbed for his gun. Kilkenny snapped a shot and the man staggered back, grabbing at his arm. A shot ripped past Kilkenny, scarring the pommel of his saddle as he lunged forward. He snapped another shot, then raced the buckskin between Nita's house and the Border Bar, dropping from the saddle.

He was up the back steps in two jumps, and had swung open the door. Firing had broken out in front, but Kilkenny's sudden attack from the rear of the bar astonished the defenders so much that he was inside the door before they realized what was happening. He snapped a shot at a lean, red-faced gunman in the door. The fellow went down, grabbing at his chest.

The bartender made a grab at the sawed-off shotgun under the bar, and Kilkenny took him with his left-hand gun, getting off two shots. A third man let out a yelp and went out the front door, fast.

Jaime Brigo sat very still, his chair tipped back against the wall. He just watched Kilkenny, his eyes expressionless.

Kilkenny reloaded his pistols.

"Brigo," he said abruptly, "there are some men among us who would harm the *señorita*. Lem Calkins, and his brothers and sons. They would burn this place, and kill her. You savvy?"

"*Sí, señor.*"

"I must go up on the cliff. You must watch over the *señorita*."

Jamie Brigo got up. He towered above Kilkenny, and he smiled. "Of course, *señor*. I know *Señor* Calkins well. He is a man who thinks himself a good man, but he is cruel. He is also dangerous, *señor*."

"If necessary, take the *señorita* away. I shall be back when I have seen the man on the cliff."

The firing was increasing in intensity.

"You have seen Steve Lord?" Kilkenny asked Brigo.

"*Sí*. He went before you to the cliff. The *señorita* would not see him. He was very angry, and said he would return soon."

Kilkenny walked to a point just inside the window of the bar and out of line with it. For a time he studied the street. The bulk of the outlaws seemed to be holed up in the livery stable, and they were throwing out a hot fire. Some of the defenders were firing from the pile of stones beyond the town, and others from the bunkhouse. There was no way to estimate their numbers.

Some of the attacking party had closed in and got into position where they could fire into the face of the building. But for a time at least it looked like a stalemate.

Walking to the back door of the bar, Kilkenny slipped out into the yard and walked over to Buck. Safely concealed by the bar building, he was out of the line of fire of the defenders. Suddenly he heard a low call and, glancing over, saw Nita standing under the roses. An instant he hesitated, then walked over, leading Buck. For a moment he was exposed, but appeared to get by unseen.

Briefly he told her of Lem Calkins. She nodded.

"I expected that. He hates me."

"Why?" Kilkenny asked.

"Oh, because I'm a woman, I think. But he came here once, and had to be sent away. He seemed to think I was somewhat different than I am."

"I see."

"You are going to the cliff?" Her eyes were wide and dark.

"Yes."

"Be careful. There are traps up there, spring guns, and other things."

"I'll be careful."

He swung into saddle and loped the buckskin away, keeping the buildings between him and the firing.

When he cleared her house, a shot winged past him from the

135

stone pile, but he slipped behind a hummock of sand and let the buckskin run. He was going to have to work fast.

Skirting the rocks, he worked down to the stream and walked Buck into it, then turned upstream. The water was no more than a foot deep, flowing over a gravel bottom, clear and bright. For a half mile he walked the horse upstream, then turned up on the bank, and followed a weaving course through a dense thicket of willows that slowly gave way to pine and cedar. After ten minutes more of riding, he rode out on a wide plateau.

Using a high, thumb-shaped butte for a marker, he worked higher and higher among the rocks until he was quite sure he was above and behind the cliff house. Then he dismounted, and dropped the bridle over Buck's head.

"You take care of yourself, Buck," he said quietly. "I've got places to go."

Leaving his carbine in its scabbard, he left the horse and walked down through the rocks toward the cliff edge.

The view was splendid. Far below he could see the scattered houses of Apple Cañon, all of them silent in the morning sun. There were only a few. Around the cluster of buildings that made the town, there were occasional puffs of smoke. From up here he could see clearly what was happening below. The defenders were still holding forth in the livery stable and bunkhouse, and apparently in Sadler's house. His own attacking party had fanned out until they had a line of riflemen across the pass and down close to the town. They were fighting as the plan had been, shrewdly and carefully, never exposing themselves.

Kilkenny had worked out that plan himself. He was quite sure from what he had learned, and from what Rusty and a couple of others who knew Apple Cañon had told him, that the well across from Nita's house was the only source of water. That one bucket was empty, he knew, for it lay there beside the well, and alongside of it the gun that had fallen from the man's hand after Kilkenny had shot him. There were a lot of men defending Apple Cañon, and it was going to be a hot day. If they could be held there, and kept from getting water, and, if during that time he could eliminate Royal Barnes, there would be chance of complete surrender on the part of the rustlers. He believed he could persuade Steele and Frame to let them go if they surrendered as a body and left the country. His only wish was to prevent any losses among his own men while breaking up the gang.

Suddenly, even as he watched, a man dashed from the rear of the bunkhouse and made a run for the well and the fallen bucket. He was halfway to the well before a gun spoke. Kilkenny would have known that gun in a million. It was Mort Davis who was firing.

The runner sprawled face down in the dust. That would keep them quiet for a while. Nobody would want to die that way. It was at least six hundred feet to the floor of the valley from where Kilkenny stood. Remembering his calculations, he figured it would be at least fifty feet down to the cliff house and the window he had chosen. Undoubtedly there was an exit back somewhere not far from his horse, or at least somewhere among the boulders and crags either on top or behind the cliff. There had to be at least two exits. But there wasn't time to look for them now.

He had taken his rope from the saddle, and now he made it fast around the trunk of a gnarled and ancient cedar. Then he dropped it over the cliff. Carefully he eased himself over the edge and got both hands on the rope. Then, his feet hanging free, he began to lower himself. His hands gave him no trouble.

He was halfway down when the first shot came, followed by a yell. The shot was from the livery stable, and it clipped the rock wall he was facing. His face was stung with fragments of stone.

Immediately his own men opened up with a hot fire, and he

lowered himself a bit more, then glanced down looking for the window. He saw it. A little to the right.

Another shot clipped close to him, but obviously whoever was shooting was taking hurried shots without proper aim or he would not have missed. He was just thanking all the gods that the men behind the stone pile hadn't spotted him when he heard a yell, and almost instantly a shot cut through his sleeve and stung his arm. Involuntarily he jerked, and almost lost his hold. Then, as bullets began to spatter around him, he found a foothold on the window sill, and hurriedly dropped inside.

Instantly he slipped out of line with the window and froze. There was no sound from inside. Only the rattle of rifle fire down below.

The room he was in was a bedroom, empty. It was small, comfortable, and the Indian blankets spread on the bed matched those on the wall. There was a crude table and a chair.

Kilkenny tiptoed across the room and put his hand on the knob. Then slowly he eased open the door.

A voice spoke.

"Come in, Kilkenny!"

Chapter Eighteen

Quietly Kilkenny swung the door open and stepped into the room, poised to go for a gun.

A man sat in a chair at a table on which there was a dish of fruit. The man wore a white shirt, a broad leather belt, gray trousers that had been neatly pressed, and were tucked into cowhide boots. He also wore crossed gun belts and two guns. He was clean-shaven except for a small mustache, and there was a black silk scarf about his neck. It was Victor Bonham.

"So," Kilkenny said thoughtfully, "it's you."

"That's right. Bonham or Barnes, whichever you prefer. Most people call me Royal Barnes."

"I've heard of you."

"And I've heard of you."

Royal Barnes stared at him, his eyes white and ugly. There was grim humor in them, too. "You're making trouble for me again," Barnes said.

"Again?" Kilkenny lifted an eyebrow.

"Yes. You killed the Webers. They were a bungling lot, but they were kinfolk, and people seem to think I should kill you because you killed them. I expect that's as good a reason as any."

"Mebbe."

"You were anxious to die, to come in that way."

"Safer than another way, I think," Kilkenny drawled.

Royal Barnes's eyes sharpened. "So? Somebody talks, do

they? Well, it was time I got new men, anyway. You see, Kilkenny, you're a fool. This isn't going to stop me. This is merely a setback. Oh, I grant you it is going to cause me to recruit a new bunch of men. But this will rid me of some of your men, too. Some of the most dangerous men in the Live Oak country will be killed today. The next time, it will be easier. And, you see, I intend to come back, to reorganize, and to carry on with my plans. I'd have succeeded already but for you. Steele will fight, but if he isn't killed today, I'll have him killed within the week. The same for Frame and your friend, Gates. Gates isn't dangerous alone, but he might find someone else to work with, someone as dangerous as you."

The sound of firing had grown in tempo now, but Royal Barnes did not let his eyes shift one instant. He was cool, casual, but wary as a crouched tiger. In the quiet, well-ordered room away from the confusion below, he seemed like someone from another world. Only his eyes showed what was in him.

"You seen Steve Lord?" demanded Kilkenny.

"Lord?" Barnes's eyes changed a little. "He never comes here."

"He worked with you," Kilkenny flatly accused.

Barnes shrugged carelessly. "Of course. I had to use what tools I could find. I held Nita out to him as bait, and power. I told him I would give him the Steele Ranch. He is a fool."

Slowly Kilkenny reached for cigarette papers and began building a smoke, his fingers poised and careful. "You're wrong, Barnes. Steve is crazy. He's crazy with blood lust and a craving for power. He killed Des King. He killed Sam Carter and a half dozen other men. Now he's gunnin' for you, Barnes."

Royal Barnes sat up. "Are you tellin' the truth?" he demanded. "Steve Lord killed those men?"

Kilkenny quietly told him of all that had transpired. Outside, the shooting had settled to occasional shots, no more. A break was coming, and the tension was mounting with every second.

"Now," Kilkenny added, "if you want my hunch, I think Steve figgers to get you. He figgers with you gone, he'll be king bee around here."

Royal Barnes got up, and, for a moment, he stood listening.

"Somebody's on the trail now," he said suddenly.

That would be Steve. Instantly it came to Kilkenny with startling awareness that Barnes was waiting for something, some sound, some signal. If there was a spring gun on the main trail, it would stop Steve in his tracks.

He drew deeply on his cigarette. Somewhere he could hear water dripping slowly, methodically, as though counting off the seconds. Royal Barnes dropped a hand to the deck of cards on the table, and idly riffled them. The spattering sound of the flipping cards was loud in the room.

A heavy crash sounded again. That would be Mort Davis. Somebody else trying to get water. Somebody who wouldn't try again.

Gravel rattled on the trail, and Kilkenny saw Royal Barnes's face tighten.

Then in the almost complete silence: *Bang!*

Royal Barnes dropped into a crouch and went for his gun with a sweeping movement. At the same instant, he dumped over the table and sent it crashing toward Kilkenny.

Kilkenny sprang aside barely in time to escape the table, and a shot crashed into the wall behind him. His own gun was out, and he triggered it twice with lightning-like rapidity. Through the smoke he could see Royal Barnes's eyes blazing with white light, and his lips parted in a snarl of killing fury.

Then the whole room was swept up in a crashing roar of guns. Something hit him and he was smashed back against the wall. His own guns were bucking and leaping in his hands, and he could see bright orange stabs of flame shot through with crimson streaks. He stepped forward and left, then again left, then back right, and moving in. Barnes had sprung backward through a doorway, and Kilkenny crossed the room, thumbing cartridges into his six-guns.

He went through the door with a leap. A bullet smashed the wall behind him and another tugged sharply at his sleeve. He stepped over, saw Barnes, and fired. The flame blossomed from Barnes's gun and Kilkenny felt his legs give way as he went to his knees. Barnes was backing away, his eyes wide and staring.

Slowly, desperately Kilkenny pulled himself erect and tried to get a gun up. Finally he did, and fired again, but Barnes was gone. Stumbling into the next room, he glared about. He was sick, felt himself weaving on his feet, and blood was running into his eyes.

The room was empty. Then a shot crashed behind him. He turned in a loose, stumbling circle and opened up with both guns on a weaving target. Then he felt himself falling, and he went down, hard.

He must have blacked out briefly, for when he opened his eyes he could smell the acrid smell of gunpowder, and it all came back with a rush. He turned over, and drew his knees under him. Then, catching the door frame, he pulled himself erect.

Royal Barnes, his face bloody and ugly, was propped against the wall opposite, his lips curved back in a snarl. A bullet had gone through one cheek, entering below the nose and coming out under the ear lobe. Blood was flowing down his side. Blood was soaking his shirt, too. Barnes was cursing slowly, monotonously, horribly.

"You got me," he mouthed viciously, "but I'm killin' you, too, Kilkenny."

His gun swung up, and Kilkenny's own guns bucked in his hands. He saw Barnes wince and jerk, and the bloody face twisted in pain. Then the outlaw lunged out from the wall, staggering forward, his guns roaring a crescendo of hatred as he reeled toward Kilkenny. His shooting was wild, insane, desperate, and the shots went every which way.

He was toe to toe with Kilkenny when Kilkenny finished it. He finished it with four shots, two from each gun, at three-foot range, pumping the heavy .45 slugs into the outlaw. Barnes fell, and tumbled across Kilkenny's feet.

For what seemed a long time, Kilkenny stood erect, his guns dangling, empty. He stood staring blankly above the dead man at his feet, staring at the curious pattern of the Indian blanket across the room. He could feel his breath coming in great gasps, he could feel the warm blood on his face, and he could feel his growing weakness.

Then suddenly he heard a sound. He had dropped one of his guns. Abruptly he let go of everything and fell headlong to the floor, lying there across Royal Barnes, the warm sunlight falling across his bloody face and hair. . . .

CHAPTER NINETEEN

A long, long time later he felt hands touching him, and felt his own hand reaching for his gun. A big man loomed over him, and he was trying to get his gun up when he heard a woman's voice, speaking softly. Something in him listened, and he let go the gun. He seemed to feel water on his face, and pain throbbing through him like a live thing. Then he went all away again.

When he finally opened his eyes, he was lying on a wide bed in a sunlit room. Outside there were lilacs, and he could hear a bird singing. There was a flash of red, and a redbird flitted past the window.

The room was beautiful. It was a woman's room, quiet, neat, and smelling faintly of odors he seemed to remember from boyhood. He was still lying there when a door opened and Nita came in.

"Oh, you're awake." Nita laughed, and her eyes grew soft. "We had begun to believe you'd never come out of it."

"What happened?" he mumbled.

"You were badly hit. Six times, in all. Only one of them serious. Through the body. There was a flesh wound in your leg, and one in your shoulder."

"Barnes?" Kilkenny asked quickly.

"He's dead. He was almost shot to pieces."

Kilkenny was quiet. He closed his eyes and lay still for a few minutes, remembering. In all his experience he had never known any man with such vitality. He rarely missed, and even in the hectic and confused battle in the cliff house he knew he had scored many hits. Yet Royal Barnes had kept shooting, kept fighting.

He opened his eyes again. "Steve Lord?"

"He was killed by a spring gun. A double-barreled shotgun loaded with soft lead pellets. He must have been killed instantly."

"The outlaw gang?"

"Wiped out. A few escaped in the last minutes, but not many. Webb Steele was wounded, but not badly. He's up and around. Has been for three days."

"Three days?" Kilkenny was incredulous. "How long have I been here?"

Nita smiled. "You've been very ill. The fight was two weeks ago."

Kilkenny lay quietly for a while, absorbing that. Then he remembered.

"But Calkins?"

"He was killed. Jaime killed him, and two of his family. Steele put it up to the other Calkins boys to leave me alone and to leave Jaime alone or fight him and all the ranchers. They backed down."

The two weeks more that Kilkenny spent in bed drifted by slowly, and at the end he became restless, worried. He lay in Nita Riordan's bed in her house, cared for by her, and receiving visits daily from Rusty and Tana, from Webb Steele, Frame, and some of the others. Even Lee Hall had come by to thank him. But he was restless. He kept thinking of Buck, and remembering the long, lonely trails.

Then one morning he got up early. Rusty and Tana had come in the night before. He saw their horses in the corral when he went out to saddle Buck.

The sun was just coming up and the morning air was cool and soft. He could smell the sagebrush and the mesquite blossoms. He felt restless and strange. Instinctively he knew he faced a crisis more severe than any brought on by his gunfight. Here, his life could change, but would it be best?

"I don't know, Buck," he said thoughtfully. "I think we'd better take a ride and think it over. Out there in the hills where the wind's in a man's face, he can think better."

He turned at the sound of a footstep, and saw Nita standing behind him. She looked fresh and lovely in a print dress, and her eyes were soft. Kilkenny looked away quickly, and cursed himself under his breath for his sudden weakness.

"Are you going, Kilkenny?" she asked.

He turned slowly. "I reckon, Nita. I reckon out there in the hills a man can think a sight better. I got things to figger out."

"Kilkenny," Nita asked suddenly, "why do you talk as you do? You can speak like an educated man when you wish. And you were, weren't you? Tana told me she picked up a picture you dropped once, a picture of your mother, and there was an inscription on it, something about it being sent to you in college."

"Yes, I reckon I can speak a sight better at times, Nita. But I'm a Western man at heart, and I speak the way the country does." He hesitated, looking at her somberly. "I reckon I better go now."

There were tears in Nita's eyes, but she lifted her head and smiled at him.

"Of course, Kilkenny. Go, and if you decide you want to come back . . . don't hesitate. And, Buck"—she turned quickly to the long-legged horse—"if he starts back, you bring him very fast, do you hear?"

For an instant, Kilkenny hesitated again, then he swung into saddle.

The buckskin wheeled, and they went out of Apple Cañon at a brisk trot. Once he looked back, and Nita was standing where he had left her. She lifted her hand and waved.

He waved in return, then faced away to the west. The wind from over the plains, fresh with morning, came to his nostrils, and he lifted his head. The buckskin's ears were forward, and he was quickening his pace.

"You an' me, Buck," Kilkenny said slowly, "we ain't civilized. We're wild, and we belong to the far, open country where the wind blows and a man's eyes narrow down to distance."

Kilkenny sat sideward in the saddle and rolled a smoke. Then his voice lifted, and he sang:

> *I have a word to say, boys, only one to say,*
> *Don't never be no cow thief, don't never ride no*
>   *stray.*
> *Be careful of your rope, boys, and keep it on the tree,*
> *But suit yourself about it, for it's nothing at all to me!*

He sang softly, and the hoofs of the buckskin kept time to the singing, and Lance could feel the air in his face, and a long way ahead the trail curved into the mountains.

ABOUT THE AUTHOR

Louis Dearborn LaMoore (1908–1988) was born in Jamestown, North Dakota. He left home at fifteen and subsequently held a wide variety of jobs although he worked mostly as a merchant seaman. From his earliest youth, L'Amour had a love of verse. His first published work was a poem, "The Chap Worth While", appearing when he was eighteen years old in his former hometown's newspaper, the *Jamestown Sun*. It is the only poem from his early years that he left out of *Smoke From This Altar* that appeared in 1939 from Lusk Publishers in Oklahoma City, a book that L'Amour self-published. However, this poem is reproduced in *The Louis L'Amour Companion* (Andrews and McMeel, 1992) edited by Robert Weinberg. L'Amour wrote poems and articles for a number of small circulation arts magazines all through the early 1930s and, after hundreds of rejection slips, finally had his first story accepted, "Anything for a Pal" in *True Gang Life* (10/35). He returned in 1938 to live with his family where they had settled in Choctaw, Oklahoma, determined to make writing his career. He wrote a fight story bought by Standard Magazines that year and became acquainted with editor Leo Margulies who was to play an important rôle later in L'Amour's life. "The Town No Guns Could Tame" in Popular Publications' *New Western* (3/40) was his first published Western story.

During the Second World War, L'Amour was drafted and ultimately served with the U.S. Army Transportation Corps in

Europe. However, in the two years before he was shipped out, he managed to write a great many adventure stories for Standard Magazines. The first story he published in 1946, the year of his discharge, was a Western, "Law of the Desert Born", in *Dime Western* (4/46). A call to Leo Margulies resulted in L'Amour's agreeing to write Western stories for the various Western pulp magazines published by Standard Magazines, a third of which appeared under the byline Jim Mayo. The proposal for L'Amour to write new Hopalong Cassidy novels came from Margulies who wanted to launch *Hopalong Cassidy's Western Magazine* to take advantage of the popularity William Boyd's old films and new television series were enjoying with a new generation. Doubleday & Company agreed to publish the pulp novelettes in hard cover books. L'Amour was paid $500 a story, no royalties, and he was assigned the house name Tex Burns. L'Amour read Clarence E. Mulford's books about the Bar-20 and based his Hopalong Cassidy on Mulford's original creation. Only two issues of the magazine appeared before it ceased publication. Doubleday felt that the Hopalong character had to appear exactly as William Boyd did in the films and on television, and thus even the first two novels had to be revamped to meet with this requirement prior to publication in book form.

L'Amour's first Western novel under his own byline was *Westward the Tide* (World's Work, 1950). It was rejected by every American publisher to which it was submitted. World's Work paid a flat £75 without royalties for British Empire rights in perpetuity. L'Amour sold his first Western short story to a slick magazine a year later, "The Gift of Cochise", in *Collier's* (7/5/52). Robert Fellows and John Wayne purchased screen rights to this story from L'Amour for $4,000, and James Edward Grant, one of Wayne's favorite screenwriters, developed a script from it, changing L'Amour's Ches Lane to Hondo Lane. L'Amour retained the right to novelize Grant's screenplay, which differs substantially from his short story, and he was able to get an endorsement from Wayne to be used as a blurb, stating that *Hondo* was the finest Western Wayne had ever read. *Hondo* (Fawcett Gold Medal, 1953) by Louis L'Amour was released on the same day as the film, *Hondo* (Warner, 1953), with a first printing of 320,000 copies.

With *Showdown at Yellow Butte* (Ace, 1953) by Jim Mayo, L'Amour began a series of short Western novels for Don Wollheim that could be doubled with other short novels by other authors in Ace Publishing's paperback two-fers. Advances on these were $800, and usually the author never earned any royalties. *Heller With a Gun* (Fawcett Gold Medal, 1955) was the first of a series of original Westerns L'Amour had agreed to write under his own name following the success of *Hondo* for Fawcett. L'Amour wanted even this early to have his Western novels published in hard cover editions. He rewrote "Guns of the Timberland" by Jim Mayo in *West* (9/50) to produce *Guns of the Timberlands* (Jason Press, 1955), a hard cover Western for which he was paid an advance of $250. Another novel for Jason Press followed, and then *Silver Canyon* (Avalon Books, 1956) for Thomas Bouregy & Company. These were basically lending library publishers, and the books seldom earned much money above the small advances paid.

The great turn in L'Amour's fortunes came about because of problems Saul David was having with his original paperback Westerns program at Bantam Books. Fred Glidden had been signed to a contract to produce two original paperback Luke Short Western novels a year for an advance of $15,000 each. It was a long-term contract, but, in the first ten years of it, Fred Glidden only wrote six novels. Literary agent Marguerite E. Harper then persuaded Bantam that Fred's brother, Jon, could help fulfill the contract, and Jon was signed for eight Peter Dawson Western novels. When Jon died suddenly before completing even one book for Bantam, Harper managed to engage a ghost writer at the Disney studios to write these eight "Peter Dawson" novels, beginning with *The Savages* (Bantam, 1959). They proved inferior to anything Jon Glidden had ever written, and what sales they had seemed to be due only to the Peter Dawson name.

Saul David wanted to know from L'Amour if *he* could deliver two Western novels a year. L'Amour said he could, and he did. In fact, by 1962 this number was increased to three original paperback novels a year. The first L'Amour novel to appear under the Bantam contract was *Radigan* (Bantam, 1958).

The strategy Bantam Books used in marketing L'Amour was to keep all of his Western titles continuously in print. Independent distributors were required to buy titles in lots of 10,000 copies if they wanted access to other Bantam titles at significantly discounted prices. In time L'Amour's paperbacks forced almost everyone else off the racks in the Western sections. L'Amour himself comprised the other half of this successful strategy. He dressed up in cowboy outfits, traveled about the country in a motor home, visiting with independent distributors, taking them to dinner and charming them, making them personal friends. He promoted himself at every available opportunity. L'Amour insisted that he was telling the stories of the people who had made America a great nation, and he appealed to patriotism as much as to commercialism in his rhetoric.

There are many fine, and some spectacular, moments in Louis L'Amour's Western fiction. He was perhaps at his best in his magazine stories. Certainly these stories possess several of the characteristics in purest form that account in largest measure for the loyal following Louis L'Amour won from his readers: a strong male character who is single and hence marriageable; and the powerful, romantic, strangely compelling vision of the American West that invests his Western fiction and makes it such a delight—in L'Amour's words: "It was a land where nothing was small, nothing was simple. Everything, the lives of men and the stories they told, ran to extremes." Louis L'Amour's next Five Star Western will be *A Man Called Trent*.